Bernard Ashley spent time in the RAF before training to be a teacher, specializing in drama. He went on to work as a head teacher for thirty years and now writes full time. His first novel, *The Trouble with Donovan Croft*, won the 'Other Award. Since then he has been shortlisted for the Carnegie Medal three times, as well as the Guardian Children's Fiction Prize.

Bernard loves the theatre and has also written for the stage and for television. The children's TV series *Dodgem*, which he adapted from his own novel, won the Royal Television Society award for best children's entertainment programme in 1993.

Bernard is married with three sons and four grandchildren and lives in Charlton, south east London.

SMOKE SCREEN

First published in the UK in 2006 by Usborne Publishing Ltd.,
Usborne House, 83-85 Saffron Hill, London EC1N 8RT, England.
www.usborne.com

This is a work of fiction. The characters, incidents, and dialogues are
products of the author's imagination and are not to be construed as real.
Any resemblance to actual events or persons, living or dead, is entirely
coincidental.

A CIP catalogue record for this book is available from the
British Library.

JFMAM JASOND/06   ISBN 0 7460 6791 7   Printed in Great Britain.

SMOKE SCREEN

BERNARD ASHLEY

USBORNE

CHAPTER ONE

Zlatko Matesa stood facing the bark of the tree, killing
a line of ants with the fingers of his free hand. Between his
thin lips smouldered a foul smelling cigarette, which he
took out and doused before he zipped up his trousers. His
face was expressionless, pale skin, dark hair cut short, and
when he revealed them, very good teeth that looked as if
he could bite hard. He turned towards the river, looked at
his watch, and pulled his mobile phone from his pocket.

To the second, the phone rang. He listened, didn't utter more than a growl, and finally seemed to be satisfied about something. With the curtest of nods – nothing as weak as a smile – he snapped the phone shut and headed back to the clearing where he'd parked the van.

He bumped through the track in the woods to the D45 and steered onto the quiet French road, where his sudden acceleration told the world that another deal had been done.

Ellie Searle was by her own stretch of water, on the towpath of the Regent's Canal in London. She was on the long bend where the canal ran through the final lock before opening out into Limehouse Basin, a girl alone, staring at the sluggish water. She hated the water, she hated the sound of it as it forced its way between the crack of the closed lock gates, as it ran over the weir beyond; she hated the sight of it; and she hated the fact of it. After what had happened in her life she had a deep mistrust of what water could do – and now she couldn't believe what was happening to her.

Her father was bringing her to live beside a canal. How cruel was that? Or selfish? Or, at its best, just how thoughtless and inconsiderate? He had to know how she felt about water.

hardened not to show much emotion except having a laugh, or dishing out tough justice against drugs on the premises; and Ellie knew that in a few years she could be in her mother's shoes, serving behind the bar, and that girls growing up in pubs don't have soft edges – dry eyes come with the job, and private thoughts and feelings go cellar deep inside. As a pub kid you're spoiled by the regulars but you don't buy it, you know the meaning of every foul word but you don't use them, and you need your sleep but you rarely get to bed before closing time. All of which had happened fast for Ellie Jane Searle.

Her father was an ex-footballer, Chris Searle, son of the great international Danny, who'd lifted more cups than most. At the end of his own less distinguished career, Ellie's father had gone into the brewery trade as a trainee manager with Bass, and in time he had taken his own tenancy – just as Ellie's mother died in that terrible accident. So for the past months the Cherry Tree at Charlton had been *their* thing, Chris's and Ellie's, father and daughter. There was a morning cleaner, a midday cook, casual bar staff, a weekend potman, and Ellie helping on the computer with the accounts – and busy in the kitchen with the microwave on Charlton Athletic home game Saturdays. Ellie lived a pub life.

After the tragic death of her mother and with school and the Cherry Tree, Ellie had no time for tears; none left for shedding, anyway. Except when all that came to an end.

'Head up, Babe, we'll come an' see you!'

'Can't lose touch with a soul sister...'

Two of Ellie's best mates were leaning over her, patting and stroking with the hands that weren't holding their mobiles.

Ellie snuffled and came up off the desk, digging for a tissue. 'Yeah,' she said, the kid with the brave face again. 'Sure.' But she knew they wouldn't stay friends for long. Charlton on the south side of the river was a universe away from the East End where she was going. People never crossed to the other side of the Thames unless they really had to. Even her footballer father, cheered in south London and Kent, would be just a name painted over a pub door in Limehouse. Over the door of the Regent's Arms.

The 'Regent' was a pub that should have been good news because it was Chris Searle's own, where he wasn't going in as a manager or on a brewery tenancy, but where he owned the premises from the cellar floor to the Sky dish on the chimney pot. It had been left to him in the will of a great-uncle he'd not seen as much of as he should: Uncle Ronnie Lewis, an old footballer himself, Arsenal,

Millwall, Dover and finally Faversham. With the previous deaths of a few in-betweens the pub had come to Chris, lock, stock and metal cask: and it was a unique set-up, because it fronted onto the Regent's Canal at Limehouse.

In Venice they would have been millionaires, but the Regent's Canal isn't the Laguna. And as for the pub, the place was old, and damp, and badly needed doing up. It had once been a lock-keeper's house, with a small untidy garden at the side, but everything had been let go. Worst of all, Ellie would have to change schools, change boroughs, change *cultures* to come and live here. And the pub looked like a real money loser. On the day she first saw it, with the wife of a friend of old Uncle Ronnie running the place, it hardly sold three pints of lager in two hours: there'd be no living made out of that.

But her dad already had a light in his eyes. They had driven through the Blackwall Tunnel, turned left, and parked at Limehouse Basin, a large marina filled with yachts and barges and surrounded by shining smart apartment blocks. The new aristocracy lived here, the successful actors, designers, the City people, personalities in public life who spent their weekends in the country or out on the water. And from here it was just a few steps along the canal towpath to the Regent's Arms.

'Brill!' her dad said. He paced his way through the old plush bar to the brick-built outhouse at the side.

'Future! Potential!' – asking for a coffee from old Annie behind the bar. 'Have we got a catering licence?' he wanted to know.

'I'll do you egg an' chips.'

'Cheers, no; but *can* you?'

'I told you, I'll do you egg and chips, an' I won't break the yellow. I say what I mean an' I mean what I say...'

'No, what *I* mean is, are we *allowed* to serve food here?' Chris persisted. 'Do the health people come? Are we licensed for grub?'

'Must be,' the old woman said. ''Cos I'll always knock up a sarnie if someone's hungry. 'Ow about the girlie? You want a bite, too, love?'

Ellie shook her head. 'No, ta.' It was a late spring day, quite warm, and the door onto the canal towpath was open. She got up and dragged herself outside, stole a look at the lock with the water spilling through, and across at the weir that ran alongside it; and she shivered. Now she was going to have to live here, and move school, no longer be the old Ellie Searle with a place in the school pecking order, and when she thought about it – trying not to be a drama queen – go through the next worse time in her life to the death of her mother.

But all her dad was doing was rubbing his hands and dreaming about his plans – 'moving on': in the car, and back at the old place, and locking up that night after he'd called time. 'You saw them apartments, all them posh properties, those expensive yachts and barges in the Basin. And what's there? Old heritage pubs along the river front and a couple of smartish restaurants.'

'So?'

'So what's going to go down a treat for the rich residents, right on their doorstep? A bit of choice for the admirals and captains on the water, and the London "goers"? Where's the gap in the market? Eh? I'll tell you, a smart canal-side restaurant: clear the garden, tables outside, decent food, reasonable prices, good midday trade and a candlelit atmosphere for night-time. Drinks, yes, up at the bar or at your table – but good food, not your usual pub stuff, cooked by a real chef with high standards. "The 'in' place to eat out..."' He ran the slogan in the air with his hand.

Ellie saw the look on her father's face and wanted, wanted, wanted never to see it go, the burning light of the dreamer, something that had been snuffed out when Mum had died: it was as if he was about to turn a corner. But Ellie Searle would have to turn the corner with him, and she was desperately unhappy about that.

Besides, he was talking rubbish! 'You're going to pay a chef? What with?' She did the accounts, she'd seen the books. 'Bank of Toyland money?'

There was no taking the shine off his apple, though.

'I'll learn, I'll be my own Jamie Oliver. Yeah, get someone proper to start with, contract for a season, then I'll take over. You can learn these things. Your mum was a good cook, we've got the books an' we'll get more. Start small, yes, but shut the Regent for a couple of weeks while we redo the inside – and we go for it!'

'Hang on! What about plan B?' Ellie was making them both a cocoa, her back to her father, kitchens being a good place to talk tough because you don't have to face the opposition. 'Plan B's favourite...'

'What's plan B?' Chris was cashing up the Cherry Tree's night, putting the notes from the till into the large floor safe tucked under a work surface.

'You sell the old Regent and carry on here. I'm doing okay at school, and we're doing all right here as tenants.' The Cherry Tree had a small, regular clientele from the streets around, the cash turnover wasn't brilliant but they were holding their own amongst other Charlton pubs, and home football games always gave a boost – the Charlton Athletic 'faithful' had adopted it. If the brewers ever shut the Cherry Tree they'd be shutting everything outside the town centres. 'Else you could give this up and find yourself saddled with a loser.'

'Could do.' Chris slammed the safe door shut and gave the combination a spin. He came over and took his cocoa, stirred it till it was almost whipped, finding the words in the swirl. 'Listen, Ellie, I went to eight different schools, following Granddad's transfers – you do that when your dad's a top footballer – changing school's not the end of the world, you look on it as an education in itself. You'll cope, you know you can; on my life, I wouldn't do this if you couldn't cope.' He took a sip. 'Lovely.' He paused, then deep in his throat he said, 'And I can just see Mum looking down and saying...' he took another mouthful of hot cocoa, gave his eyes an excuse for watering up, '..."Go for it, Chrissie. Take the chance. Be yourself."'

Ellie looked at her father, didn't blink. 'That's crap!' she said. 'Mum's dead – and she won't ever come back.' Now Ellie had a catch in her own throat. 'But if you want it enough to come all that sob stuff on me, I s'pose you'll have to do it.'

And she went to bed – to see again in her head the picture of her mother, lying dead, an imaginary picture that would never go.

It was instant attraction. It can happen like that, the friendship version of falling in love. It was the first day of the new term at the new school and Ellie's consolation prize was there in place, sitting next to her at a double desk in the form room: a girl called Flo Moses.

That morning Ellie had felt as raw as the new Year

Sevens in the school yard of Limehouse High, her bright new scarlet sweatshirt still smelling of its plastic wrapping as she'd tacked onto the back of the 9L line. But a corridor jostle's a corridor jostle whether you're old, new, supply teacher or deputy head; a school corridor's a great leveller, and Ellie Searle could always barge her weight; so by the time she'd squeezed through the form-room door her newness was well creased.

She sat where there was a spare place, slung her bag onto the desk and folded her arms on it, waiting for whatever word was going to come from the form teacher who was sorting herself out at the front. And next to her this girl said, 'You move about a lot?'

'No. Why?' Ellie looked into a beautiful black face, a hint of make-up on the lips and eyelids.

'You've got the push of a traveller kid – in this school, in that, never fazed by what anyone's up to. No "May I?", just, "Kiss my ass!" as you come barging through that door.'

'You noticed?'

'An' most kids ask permission to sit next to me.'

'Why? Don't they know you smell?'

And that was it. The girl stared at her then screeched with a sudden laugh, Ellie joined in, and they both got ticked off for inappropriate behaviour, names on the board, first morning: blood sisters in trouble, straight off.

Which was what Ellie needed, because back home at the Regent's Arms things were dire, so much so that coming to a new school on the other side of the river had ended up way down her list of worries. But all gifts gratefully received...

She and her dad had moved during the school holiday, and that had been their summer, fitting into the Regent's Arms by the canal. Their furniture had come down the narrow steps from Salmon Lane, and they'd sorted themselves into the private accommodation while old Annie looked after the bar. It was a temporary, sort-it-later sort of move, tea chests and suitcases sitting in the middles of rooms for a few days because there was a business to run. Her dad wanted to let Ellie have the front bedroom while he faced Salmon Lane, but she didn't want the sight and the sound of the water, not yet; no, not yet, so she had the back. None of their curtains fitted here, and her old wardrobe was too big to come so she had to make do with shallow cupboards each side of a filled-in fireplace. Personal accommodation problems weren't the big headache, though. It was the business, and from the start there was going to be a battle of wills.

When Ellie's dad sat in the bar costing up the price of knocking through to the outhouse and putting in a bigger kitchen, saying something to Ellie about his closure plans, old Annie's barmaid's smile suddenly turned into a frown.

'Close up? You can't do that, guv'nor. They won't 'ave that round here!'

'Who won't have it?'

'The customers. Your regulars.'

'What regulars? We've hardly got any regulars. My Ellie's our biggest regular, drinking her Coca-Colas.'

Ellie burped to prove a point.

Annie slapped a hand flat on the bar. ''Ow long you been here?' she asked. 'Tell me, 'ow many days?'

Chris stopped the costing calculation he was doing to count on his fingers. 'Five,' he said. 'Sunday, Monday, Tuesday, Wednesday, Thursday.'

''An' you 'aven't been here tomorrow?'

'No, I 'aven't been here tomorrow. Why, what's so special about Fridays? Do we actually do more'n a tenner of business on a Friday?'

Annie slid a pint of Special along the bar to an old man with a dog, both sitting up on bar stools growling at each other.

'"Do we do more'n a tenner?" Haven't you seen the cashing up? Didn't you see Friday's takings?'

Chris might have or he might not, but Ellie had, although she'd thought that decent amount was a sort of accumulation, a total of all the weeks since old Uncle Ronnie had died.

'I'll tell you.' Annie came round the bar, took Chris's arm and led him into the kitchen. Ellie came away from the laptop where she was designing the 'Pub Closed for Refurbishment' signs to strain an ear at the door. 'Friday night is music night,' Annie went on. 'Friday night is locals' night; they all come in of a Friday. Why? 'Cos we've got the best music this side of the Circus Tavern, Friday nights. You won't stop pulling pints, Fridays – it'll 'ave your arm in a sling.'

'Straight up?'

'You never heard of Ivy Stardust your side of the river? They come from all over to hear Ivy, this side. She's your banker, guv'nor. She's your business. An' you can't shut up on her or you'll never get her back. She's got a right loyal following...'

'Never heard of her.'

'Well you wouldn't, from over Charlton! Didn't them solicitors tell you what the business is?'

'Not really.'

And Ellie, just round the woodwork, knew the truth of it. Whatever her dad had been told about the Regent's Arms, whether he knew there was sometimes a bit of music on Friday nights or not, his mind was fixed on all that being old hat, in the past. New plans for a posh venue just a stroll away from Limehouse Basin was all the man had in his head.

The stupid man!

'Have we got a licence for live music?' he asked.

'Must have. Like the grub,' Annie told him. 'I'll do you a dance for sixpence!'

'Well, we'll see.'

'You'd do best to see it their way!' Annie's voice sounded deadly serious. 'I tell you, guv'nor, don't you cross that Ivy whatever you do, not her lot. That'd be a big mistake, you mark my words!'

CHAPTER TWO

Fang Song Yin stood in the humble entrance that led into the Fuchow People's Hall, the only communal building in the village. She didn't want people to guess her secret dreams, so she came when the place was empty: not to stand on the platform and sing, but to bolster her hopes by looking at what was on the wall: those pinned white sheets of paper, with names in red calligraphy paint on them. She went from sheet to sheet

– there were ten of them – and all were filled with names except the last, the freshest, that had just the one name on it. She put a finger on the paint. It was dry, but its scarlet hadn't yet turned dark with time. She looked at the name. Hu Peng. She remembered this boy, his family farmed the sweet potato fields below her mother's, and the first year the crop had failed, he went, left the region. Now his was the one name on the new sheet, he had arrived somewhere! Song drew herself up to her one metre sixty. He could do it, so could she!

She turned from the sheet and walked out of the hall into the sun of a Chinese morning; her dream had not evaporated. She was pretty, people said, seventeen years old and with a fair singing voice. She walked down the dusty slope to her home, starting to hum to herself. Yes, she had got what was needed, the reassurance – she was determined to try to do what Hu Peng had done, and make her village proud of her.

Her humming took her to the bend in the track from where she could see her home; and suddenly she fell silent; because she knew that the next thing she had to do was to tell her mother. She had to convince her that she was old enough to do what those others with names in red paint had done, and go in search of the better life that was waiting away from Fuchow. She had stopped her humming, but as her thoughts ran on she gathered pace;

because she knew what her mother would say, the same as her dead father would have said, that what she wanted to do was more than a dream for herself: it was a dream for them all.

'A pub?' Flo was asking Ellie that first day in the dining hall. 'Beer and strong liquors?'

'And Red Squares and Breezers.'

'I'm comin' down then, your canal's not far from me. You do sleepovers?'

'Can if I want. But we never touch the drink,' Ellie told her. 'Coke or tea, and cocoa last thing, they're our weakness.'

'Aaah! Clean livers – bless! Lord, haven't I fell on my feet? New kid in school, she's all right – an' she lives in a pub!'

Ellie smiled to herself. So she was all right! That helped. But looking at Flo forking up her stringy chicken curry as if she was enjoying it – the way she took on life as it came at her – Ellie realized how little the girl knew about the fix she and her dad were in.

Because 'Friday Night is Music Night' hadn't been at all the sort of event they'd seen coming. Her dad had allowed it to go ahead, this week only, just so as to give himself the ammunition for cancelling it the next, with excuses like, not enough trade, Ivy Stardust too expensive – or just no good as a singer. Which was weak of him, Ellie thought, because he'd missed the chance to stop it from the off, to be the new broom sweeping clean. He'd let the door stay open instead of shutting it, which was always a mistake. *We'll see* usually means *yes* rather than *no*, every kid knew that.

It had started at around half past six on the Friday when the equipment came; and not by road to be humped down the awkward steps but gliding easy, along the canal. Ellie heard the shouts, the loud voices, and ran to a front window to look out over the greenish water. A small and battered cabin cruiser was there, being tied up a few metres upstream of the lock. It had a flowing 'hair in the wind' logo painted on the cabin, and *Watson Travel* with a telephone number listed alongside, showing an out-of-date dialling code. A boy a bit older than Ellie was doing the tying up to a bollard, while a big-built guy in jeans and sweatshirt was starting to carry speakers off the boat – big and heavy themselves, hefted across the towpath into the pub, one after the other, four of them, quadraphonic – with the two bigger ones needing the boy to help.

Ellie finished what she was doing and came downstairs. She'd changed out of school gear, put on a sparkly silver vest top with jeans and just a touch of make-up, Flo-style. Now she was ready to be a bit of help on the night.

Her dad was doing what he always did before expecting a crowd, like on Charlton match days; he was testing his barrels and taps, making sure he wasn't going to have to change a cask midway; and putting full bottles of spirits in the optics behind the bar. Annie was slitting open boxes of crisps with a hooked knife — and she'd changed, too. Tonight she wasn't old Annie in a cardy but the smarter 'dinner-and-dance' version in high heels and a low-cut blouse.

A platform about fifteen centimetres high had been brought in from the outhouse — and as it was being covered in a heavy black cloth by the boy from the boat, Ellie realized what it was for; it was the stage.

'You paid to watch?' the boy suddenly asked Ellie, coming up from the floor with a swear, flicking his hand in pain.

'No!'

'Then you can help, can't you? Get them creases out.' And he left her to straighten the stage cloth while he went around the room sliding tables into different positions, and throwing chairs about.

Ellie finished her job, and just got out of the way in time for a batten of footlights to be thumped on the front of the stage by the speakers man. 'Mind your arse!' he told her.

Ellie looked across for her father, but he'd gone along to the outhouse for a carton of pint glasses. Taken over! They were being taken over by these people, and Ellie felt an anger rising up inside, the sort that thins the brain somehow, just before you say something in a screech. But she didn't. Because with the anger there was something else. It was fear. She was scared – although she didn't know what about.

Everything was busy, busy, busy – without any customers yet. The Regent's Arms wasn't on a route from a station, people going home didn't drop in, there was no 'passing trade'; this time of day the place was deader than a locked-up church. But now a keyboard came in, wheeled by a miserable-looking man of about fifty – who when he took his coat off turned out to be wearing a bright blue blazer with a matching bow tie. Showbiz! He positioned his keyboard and started plugging into sockets and amps; not a word to anyone, least of all to Ellie's dad. With the bar being changed around and the music setting up, it was as if Chris Searle was hired bar help. In came a microphone on a stand, and as Ellie stood watching the hefty roadie wiring it in, the boy shouted over to her.

''Ere, you, Skinny – where's my small table?'

'You talking to me?'

'Who else?'

'The name's Ellie Searle; my dad—'

'The small table. I 'ave it by the door.'

'What small table?' Ellie could feel her gall rising, not so scared now after the sight of the sad old case in the blue blazer: real caravan site entertainment, this was going to be. And she wasn't going to be bossed about in her own pub by some yobby boy. 'Use one of the others.'

'Too big, stupid! They're for punters, audience, we get six round them.' The boy was looking around the place, behind the bar, opening the door to the private stairs.

'What's it for, then?' she asked him.

'Me. On the door. Takings. Entrance money!' he explained into her face before going on looking.

Which answered one question: how the music was paid for. Annie had said Chris would have to sort that with Ivy Stardust, and he and Ellie had reckoned she'd want a cut of the bar takings, a percentage. *How big?* was going to be the only question.

'Oi! Where are you going?' Ellie's dad had reappeared, and he was standing across the doorway into the kitchen, blocking it off from the searching boy.

'Table. I'm looking for me table.'

'*Your* table? I'm the landlord here.' Ellie could see that her dad, like her, was at that point where he wasn't going to be pushed much further, no matter what. 'I'll look you out a table if you tell me what you want.'

28

'Ronnie knew.'

'Ronnie's scattered all over the Arsenal pitch.' And Chris Searle pushed his face close to the boy's, the centre forward who's taken just about enough from a chancy defender. 'We're under new management!' he told him, thumping his own chest.

'You got a problem?'

Ellie spun round at a new voice. A woman's, hard, clear, loud. She had a coat draped round her shoulders, almost down to the floor where silver sparkly shoes peeped out. Her hair was blonde in a short, expensive cut, sparkle in it, and her face was made up with great skill. She had to be fifty or more, but she looked thirty if you didn't stare, and attractive in a fairground sort of way. It had to be the singer.

Who her question was for, wasn't clear. Did Ellie's father have the problem, or the boy?

'Ivy Stardust,' she said, slinking off her coat to show a three-quarter length, dark blue, sequinned dress.

'Chris Searle,' said Ellie's dad. 'New guv'nor.'

Ivy gave him a look up and down as she put out a hand to be taken. 'Ivy Stardust; Watson to you,' she said, with a showbiz smile.

It took Chris a moment to sort out what she'd said, that she hadn't been asking a question. 'Ah. "Stardust" is—'

'Just stardust! Stage name,' she answered, with a castanet click of her fingers and a slow blink.

Oh, no! Ellie thought. She fancies him! As if things weren't awkward enough already! And Watson! Wasn't that the name on the cabin cruiser? Was she *Watson Travel*?

'I still need a bleedin' table for the door!' the boy said.

'You'll get a kick up the jacksie, you swear at the new guv'nor!' Ivy told him. 'Go an' look in the kitchen!'

Which is what he did, without Ellie's dad stopping him this time. It seemed that Ivy Stardust ran this place on Fridays. The boy found what he wanted, a card table that Chris had tucked behind the fridge and, with a poisonous look at Ellie, the boy went to the door and set himself up with a cash tin and a roll of raffle tickets.

Meanwhile, with no more reference to the guv'nor — except saying yes to the offer of a drink, a large Baileys for the voice — Ivy went to the small stage, had a lighting check for two spotlights linked to the keyboard, and went to sit at a corner table with the other musician, Len, and the roadie.

Ellie went into the kitchen and checked the microwave, the jacket potatoes, the sandwich fillings and the margarine spread. Annie had said food wasn't on the agenda with the Friday night crowd, but Ellie was ready to be busy if need be. What you don't try, you don't get!

And at seven o'clock, the music night started.

Ellie didn't know where people came from. In no time, as if someone had opened a gate somewhere, the pub started filling up with punters, two and three deep at the bar, with Ellie's dad and Annie suddenly swinging, turning, skipping round each other like dance champions, down for bottles, along for ice, up for glasses, out for cash, while the music started playing – recorded stuff from the keyboard at first, then to a few cheers and a 'Go it, girl!' Ivy Stardust got up to sing. The digital keyboard had everything on it, different tones, the drums and bass and background rhythms, over which Ivy Stardust sang her way through the standards: Cole Porter, George Gershwin, songs from the shows, songs from the films, and a few popular hits of the past.

She certainly had her fans in; people were mainly quiet while she sang, attentive, just a couple of tables of youngish, more restless youths quietly talking on; and at the end of each number the clapping was way above polite. But in-between – and there were lots of in-betweens – the noise in the bar crept up, and the customers moved around, went to talk at different tables. People went out for a smoke, others came in, a few of the audience changed. From the kitchen door behind the bar Ellie watched them. There were young and old, some dressed up for a Friday night out, others not bothering –

all very happy with laughs and clinks and more rounds of drinks. And a very modern East End mix: middle-aged and elderly whites, a table mostly youngish Chinese, probably from where the old Chinatown used to be, some other Asians, and a few Afro-Caribbean faces. Plus that other East End element: Ellie could see them across the room, they were opposite the music, drinking spirits — five men, two of them Chinese, all in suits, who were talking among themselves, with hard expressions on their faces that would deter anyone from asking them to listen to Ivy Stardust. They gave Ellie the shivers, and she was pleased when someone asked for a sandwich and she suddenly started to get busy.

Meanwhile, having food on offer hadn't been a bad idea; one person saw the sandwich, someone else on their table fancied one, and that was the start of it. Two slices of bread, a spread of Anchor, a fork of filling, onto the plate with a serviette. Or a split in the spud, four minutes in the microwave, a wedge of Anchor, again, onto the plate with a fork and a serviette. Annie shouted the orders and Ellie saw to them. She just had time for a short break, a quick visit to the upstairs loo; where, as she looked out of the landing window, she saw the canal the way she'd not seen it before; a couple of moored narrowboats along behind the cabin cruiser and people talking, drinking, smoking on the lock-side and along the towpath. Which seemed strange to Ellie. People who lived in narrowboats could walk along from the Basin without casting-off, it was metres not miles: but, perhaps like Annie had said, they really did come from all over to hear Ivy Stardust sing.

Inside, Chris didn't pause in his serving; there was no time for getting to know his new customers, it was all go. Annie showed her worth with the speed she worked and her memory for a large round of drinks, and the till went ring, ring, ring all evening. But busy as the evening was, right at the height of it with a bar full and an hour till closing time, the digital drum suddenly rolled, a synthesized cymbal clashed, Ivy Stardust called goodnight, there was a cheer and a final round of applause, and the entertainment had stopped. And as it did, the punters went, just a few lingering, finishing drinks, one or two ordering another, but the space at the bar widening and widening. Ivy Stardust and the keyboard had literally pulled the plug.

While Ellie washed up and cleaned her surfaces, Annie and Ellie's dad loaded the dishwasher with glasses and stacked the next lot. Rude Boy at the door helped the roadie to dismantle the speakers, and the keyboard player cased his equipment, a fag dangling from his mouth, while Ivy Stardust put on her mac to become Watson again. The black cloth was folded and taken away and the platform was put back in the outhouse. Within fifteen minutes the place was pre-six-thirty.

Ellie's dad didn't stop – washing, wiping, and sorting chairs and tables. A busy night was nothing new to him, and it had been a good night for the Regent's Arms, the safe would earn its keep tonight, and Ellie fully expected Ivy Stardust to come over to her dad and hold out her hand for a percentage on top. But she didn't. She must have been happy with what the boy had taken at the entrance because she just called, 'See you next week!' from the doorway.

And Ellie's dad didn't have time to say 'yes', 'no', or 'we'll see' before she'd gone. He paid Annie for the week, and she went, too, with just a nod and a wink and a, 'Told you, guv'nor, din' I?'

And suddenly Ellie and her dad were on their own, apart from an elderly couple who'd had too much and were all over each other in the corner.

'Well, what did you think of that?' Ellie's dad asked her as she filled a kettle.

'Busy! And I told you I'd do some trade on the food once they saw it.'

'Right!' he said. 'Good stuff.' He fixed her with a goal-scorer's eye. 'But I still want to do what I want to do.'

'You do it then.'

He went back to the till, looked at the total for the

night and nodded a certain satisfaction — before he frowned. 'Notice none of the posh brigade came, none of the Basin and smart-apartments people, it was all the old East End. Well, the new old East End, if you know what I mean.'

Ellie did, but she was too tired to go into a customer breakdown right then. 'See you tomorrow,' she told him. And she went up to bed, making herself look out from the landing at the canal, empty of vessels again, just the moon's reflection in the water; and she did what she always did, a habit she'd got into and couldn't get out of.

She looked for a body floating in the water, face up.

CHAPTER THREE

He went to her school. Rude Boy from Friday night
went to Limehouse High. Ellie saw him in the yard the
next Monday morning, the same scowly, aggressive
looking yob she'd had in her pub, only now he was in a
scruffy school uniform — spitting on the tarmac with a
crowd of hangers-on, he had 'waiting to leave' written all
over his spotty forehead.

Flo saw Ellie looking at him. 'Don't think about it,

Chicken, he's bad news, Wayne Watson.'

'I'm *not* thinking about it. He was round our place on Friday night with the music. Got right up my dad's nose.'

'He would. You know who he is?'

'What, Watson? *Watson?*' Now the name hit her: of course! Ivy "Stardust" Watson! She was his mother, or an aunt, or a gran. The way the woman had slagged him off it had definitely sounded like family...

'Weazel Wayne Watson,' Flo told her. 'His mum and her lot run the coach company on the Mile End Road.'

'Do they?'

'Two or three old bangers of coaches. Why, what happened on Friday? An' what's this about music?'

Ellie told her, in instalments; some of it before the bell, more in the break, and the last part over their school dinners — this being the secret, edgy stuff about her father's plans for a smart eatery where Ivy "Stardust" Watson would be the sand in the sun oil. But it was no monologue, because through it Ellie started to find out about Flo.

Flo, she'd liked from that first morning of term. Ellie's dad had warned her: starting a new school, you don't take up with the first person who wants to be your friend, they've usually got a reason for jumping on you, like them being a sad case. But Ellie could read people, and she knew that Flo hadn't had a spare seat next to her because no one fancied it – although the actual reason took her by surprise. And it came out as easy as a stone from a cherry.

'You got to do your own thing,' Flo said, through a second helping of sponge pudding. 'You and your dad. You don't go beholdin' to no one. You want to give someone the heave, you give 'em the heave.'

'Easy to say,' Ellie put in.

'Easy to do, girl. You just do it.' Flo swivelled round and stared at a boy on the other side of the dining room, pointed at him with her spoon. He was in their form. 'Jasbinder Prabhaker. Came on real strong, Romeo and Juliet, a love to slaughter all loves, he says; but when he got you on your own up Mile End Park all he really wanted was in here...' she thumbed at her sweatshirt, '...so I told him to eat dirt.'

Ellie laughed. Smaller and a bit skinny, she'd never had groping problems. 'And it was him who used to sit next to you?' she guessed. 'Reserved seat? Last term?'

'You got it. Left room for you, Chicken, din' it?'

'My good luck.'

'Pants!' Flo ate on. 'Let him hang out to dry for a bit' – after the next long mouthful, looking across the room again – 'teach him his manners, the dishy number. Then he'll come big eyed like a good dog when I whistle. So, is your dad looking for a cook,' she asked, fresh loaded fork, 'when he gets his caff going?'

'Restaurant,' Ellie corrected.

'Whatever.'

'He does for the start. Then he's going to learn himself!' Ellie laughed. 'Can't fault him for having a go!'

Flo screeched. 'Well, I've got your answer, missus!' There was a huge light in her eyes. 'My mum. She's a trained cook, works up Oxford Street in the Marks and Sparks canteen. No problem with her cooking, I tell you...'

Ellie looked at her friend, who wouldn't have a problem with anyone's cooking, the way she got it down, although right now she was all attention on Ellie. 'Lucky old you!' Ellie said.

'And as it happens she's looking for something more local. But it'd have to be full-time, being one-parent.'

'You?'

Flo nodded. 'Little orphan Flo. Half.'

'Your mum the half you get your appetite off?' Ellie asked her.

Flo narrowed her eyes. Ellie waited, to see which way the girl would jump. A friend who could take a joke against herself was the sort Ellie liked, because she could take them, too.

'If you ate a bit more, my girl, you might put on something where it counts an' get yourself a few boy problems...'

Ellie patted Flo's spoon hand. 'I'll try,' she said. 'But right now I reckon I've got problem enough with Rude Boy Wayne Watson.'

And at the sound of his name the bad news himself just had to come stalking up behind her.

'Speak of the devil, eh? You're a little cow, in't you?' he said, standing over the girls.

'Moo!' said Ellie.

'There's you doin' food out the back, Friday night, an' no thought for someone on the door. You could've slipped me out a sarnie or a jacket spud, couldn't you?'

'Too busy, son.'

'Well, I'll tell you, you remember where your bread an' butter comes from, Friday nights! An' you start looking after me a bit or I ain't gonna be very pleased...'

Ellie turned away, to Flo's polished plate. 'Finished?' she asked.

'Yeah. Might be sick, though.'

'Won't be the food,' Ellie said as she got up and walked off out of the dining hall. But she didn't feel as confident inside as she might have sounded on the outside. Boys like Wayne Watson always want the last word, and this was his patch, here in Limehouse, not hers. Not yet, anyway.

* * *

What would he say? Would he laugh in her face, or swear at her, or would he show a sunny side and be sympathetic? Fang Song Yin ran up the slope from her house to the village square, hoping that today would be the day when he came.

They called him 'Uncle Chen'. He smiled a lot, showed his gold teeth, waved, and flashed a Rolex watch; Song had seen him often, from a distance. He came about once a month to Fuchow, from Nanjing to the north, always with his little bottle of red paint and his brush-pen. After he had finished with his red paint in the People's Hall, he would sit at a small card table in the shade of a magnolia tree and tell people what he had to offer. At a price. But then everyone knew there was a price. Hu Peng had been one to pay it, and others after, Song guessed – although the region was large, and she wouldn't know how many, and how much. In the past some of the lucky ones had done it at the expense of their communities, people putting together their savings from better times to sponsor them to go to another place and make their fortune. But that had been in the years before. Fang Song Yin's problem was that there was no money left for that, not to cover everything: just a few yen in her mother's earthen pot.

She had come up to the magnolia tree every day since her decision, and with a thrill inside she saw that today he was there, sitting like a Buddha as if he was waiting just for her! She turned, and like a deer she ran home, to get back to talk to him before he left for another village. All clumsy fingers and tight buttonholes, she changed into her best clothes – her singing dress and high-heeled shoes – and ran swiftly back to the square, to where he was still sitting, sipping at a fruit drink. He looked up.

'Uncle Chen...'

Now he smiled, and looked her up and down. He bowed his head as if he were pleased with what he was seeing. 'Your name, beautiful girl?'

'Fang Song Yin.'

'Ah.' He went on looking at her as he told her its meaning. 'Breath of flowers, fragrant carpet of grass...'

'I have a question, Uncle Chen.'

'Everyone has a question. Do I have an answer, that's the bigger question.' And he laughed and rolled on his seat like a jolly uncle.

My question is big enough, Song thought. Young people like her, whose family fields were on the wrong slopes, had only two choices in life: well, three, if they chose to stay and grow older and more miserable here. There was no social provision to help farmers in the bad years, no tiding over, no bailing out. So the young people were expected to go to one of the big, private companies' 'economic special zones' and for pitiful wages sit fitting small electronic parts into bigger electronic parts – and that was what Song was not prepared to do. Nor was she happy to fill her dead father's shoes and try to make something of their scratch of land. She was young, she was pretty, she had a singing voice the local people clapped, and which her father had told her was a special gift – and she had a dream of a life where she could use these things that she had been specially given. This China that she knew was not what she wanted for the rest of her days, till she was lined, and bent, and her voice had gone. So she was prepared to trust this man to help her go looking for a better life somewhere else.

Song put on a smile, and laughed a little. 'I am a singer,' she said, hoping that he'd heard the music in her laughter. 'I sing in the People's Hall, and I want very much to sing as a professional and to make money to send back here to my mother...' He would know that this was not a stupid wish; Fuchow was a million miles from the chance of doing anything like that on a concert stage.

The smile hadn't left Uncle Chen's face, his eyes hadn't stopped looking her over, although Song noticed that the nails of his right hand had started tapping a little dance upon the tabletop. Such power he had!

So, what would he say?

'Of course. This is possible. All things are possible.' He opened his arms and the loose Rolex slid twinkling round on his wrist. 'Once you are in Europe, all things can be arranged.'

Song took a step back, turned to look down the valley and across towards the further mountains. Europe! She had dreamed about Europe, everyone of her age dreamed about such prosperous places with lots of opportunities; but the dream always shattered when the cost was counted. Even with a passport, where would the air fare come from? And even going overland was out of the question with the favour she had to ask. Realistically, she had been thinking of Taiwan across the water.

But Uncle Chen was waving his arm towards the People's Hall, where the red painted posters hung. 'England especially is where the most success has been had.'

'Don't people need a work permit for England?' she asked.

Uncle Chen laughed again, louder than before. 'I have contacts for all that – it all gets arranged. You speak some English?'

'Some. A little.'

From his side he produced a small stool, which he swung round to place at the table. 'Sit, Fang Song Yin,' he said, 'and we will discuss the details...'

But Song didn't sit; she couldn't, yet: not before she had asked the biggest, most important question. 'I don't have much money,' she told him. 'My father is dead, and the fields also have died on us. A few yen to offer, towards the cost, that's all – but I have talent, and I would repay you. You would not be disappointed in me. Is there another way?' Song felt sick, having to plead like this; the words tasted like bile in her mouth; but even as she pleaded she saw in her mind the upturned faces that singers see, and imagined that she heard the lute introduction to a favourite song.

Uncle Chen folded his arms. Here it came, the decision. He sipped at his drink again, and put it down with delicate fingers, making her wait. 'Mostly I am paid beforehand,' he said, 'but I think someone like you, beautiful – and talented, of course,' he added, like an afterthought, 'I think you will do well for me in England.'

Song didn't quite like the way he was looking at her: but was he really saying yes? She couldn't stop the shiver from showing itself with a twitch of her body.

He saw it. 'Sit, then,' he repeated, 'and we will draw up an agreement. You will give me what you can, and I will put up the rest of the money against your house and land, and you will repay me.' Song saw him look beyond her, down to where the cluster of fields and poor dwellings were; towards her home, and her mother. 'I am a good judge. You will not let me down, I think.'

And with just the quickest look over her shoulder,

Fang Song Yin sat, knowing that she had to take the chance – for the sake of her own youth which she was determined not to let wither here. A singer needed an audience of more than a few old men and women once or twice a year; a break had to be made, she was desperate to go; people with talent had to take their chance – it was the destiny of the young. She had thought it all through, night after night. She had dreamed it: of being in Taiwan, where she would take some ordinary work while she found the best people for whom to audition – opera, concert, musical, for the chorus and then for better parts. But now in England! Where the best opportunities existed! Some in the world had changes thrust upon them, while she would gladly indebt herself for the chance to grab at change like this.

And Song shivered with excitement again, and watched while Uncle Chen drew a small black notebook and a fountain pen from out of his robes. And while he kept the smile in his voice – although she couldn't see his eyes – he said, 'Of course, I take your land if you let me down...'

Flo brought her mother to the Regent's Arms the next Friday night, quite out of the blue. Ellie's dad had decided to let the music happen again – which meant he'd done nothing, no phone calls to arrange it, no e-mails sent, and no cancellation; and because it was regular, everyone expected it. He was still planning his building alterations, had had a word with a brewery architect he knew; meanwhile he reckoned they might as well cash in on the music. He would drop some hints, was all he told Ellie, 'prepare the ground'.

Ellie had made her plans, though – for the Friday. She would definitely do some food again, the same simple stuff, no menu but cheese or ham sandwiches, and jacket potatoes; and she wouldn't serve Rude Boy unless he came to the bar and begged. *Begged.* Annie wouldn't make him pay, of course, but Ellie would put something in his sandwich to make him think twice about calling her a cow: horseradish, more or less the same colour as margarine – and spread it on so thickly it would blow his stupid head off...

Before the cabin cruiser came with the equipment she put the card table by the door so that he didn't have to ask her for it, and when the vessel tied up she busied herself away in the kitchen so there was no chance of being told to help with the getting-in. But who walked through the door before Rude Boy Wayne Watson did, at the same time as the first loudspeaker, but Flo Moses and her mother!

Flo looked great, her hair sleeked down shiny with a small scarlet flower in it, wearing a black vest top with cropped trousers. A small sequinned purse said she was girl not woman, but her mother coming up behind was definitely woman not girl. She walked in, tall and graceful, with a black fedora hat and a pinstriped suit cut city-style. Different class! Ivy Stardust, eat your heart out!

'Flo!'

'Chicken! This is my mum...'

'And this is...' But Ellie's dad was there already, meeting with Mrs. Moses' stare.

'Hi! You're Flo, and you're...'

'Madeleine Moses,' Flo's mother said.

'Chris Searle.'

'Yeah.'

They shook hands and Chris got them drinks – a Coke for Flo and a fizzy water for her mother. 'Drivin'!' she said.

'Well...' There was a moment's hesitation as another loudspeaker came hefting in, very heavy this one, for the far back corner of the room: a moment to think because neither Ellie nor Flo nor their parents quite knew the next move, except that the Searles were going to have to be very busy in a bit.

'Ellie did some food last week, that right?' Madeleine Moses suddenly asked Chris. 'An' you could be looking for a cook?'

'Could be, later on, sure, perhaps...' Her father's face told Ellie that he should have been warned about this. Ellie just shrugged.

'Well,' and now Ellie could see that Flo's mother was carrying a large Marks and Spencer's carrier bag, the sturdy sort, 'I brought some stuff and I brought an apron and I'm here to help you out. I reckoned.'

'That's very kind of you,' Chris Searle said – as Annie the barmaid walked behind him, coughed, and pinched his backside.

'Nothing fancy, but I'm quick!' Mrs. Moses said.

'Like old Ron!' said Annie.

'Well...'

'Where's the kitchen?' Madeleine Moses was moving on. But the location of the kitchen was obvious, a new electric-blue fly zapper shone out through the door behind the bar. 'Brought some prawns an' ciabatta,' she said, making for it as Wayne Watson came in from the outhouse, carrying one end of the stage platform.

'Table?' he shouted across the room at Ellie as they thumped it down.

'Use your eyes!' she shouted back. All of which happened as her dad followed Flo and her mother into the kitchen, looking back over his shoulder helplessly at Ellie as if she could sort all this, stop every aspect of his life from being taken out of his hands.

And Rude Boy *was* using his eyes. School uniforms don't do much for anyone, so his eyes were suddenly opened by Flo looking gorgeous tonight. He whistled her across the room and stuck out his tongue, waggling it.

'Pit City! Let's Flora some bread, Chicken, 'fore I throw up!' Flo dived after her mother into the kitchen, where washing their hands and spreading margarine on loaves was the hardest work Flo and Ellie did that evening — because Madeleine Moses was fast and professional; she took over the kitchen work surface solo, rippling along and back like a pianist at a concerto. So the girls hovered in a corner of the bar well away from Wayne Watson at the door, and took everything in.

Or, tried to. It was busy, like the week before, and with so many people in a small space all they really saw were the bodies that were blocking their view; until Ivy Stardust sang. Then people sat for the three-song sets, before getting up and moving about again — to the bar, to the four corners of the room, outside. Flo and Ellie sat and nursed a couple of Cokes for most of the time, avoiding any direct line of vision with Rude Boy, until near the end, baulked by bodies most of the evening, they were ready for air.

'Come on, girl, out!' Ellie said. Rude Boy had left his place at the door to go to the gents so they made a quick move and headed for the canal towpath.

'Not yours?' Flo asked as she opened her mouth and her arms to the fresher air, looking at the narrowboat moored upstream of the lock, smoke drifting from its chimney.

'No way!' Ellie looked at the vessel. They came and went, pleasure craft; and would she want to spend leisure time on water? *Any* time? Before they'd moved she'd seen the map showing the canal. The Regent's Canal was part of the Grand Union Canal and went north to the Midlands and further, all over the country. 'That boat's called *Brummie Flower*. But Ivy Stardust can't be famous in Birmingham!'

'Chicken, Ivy Stardust ain't famous anywhere. She sings like an old dear on a Christmas outing.' Flo was shimmying ahead, a model on a catwalk. 'Don' know why they make a fuss of coming to hear that one!'

'Me neither. Beats me, sounds like an auntie at a party. It's a right mystery...' Ellie looked along the towpath where the people coming out at the end of a song set made the Regent's Arms look busy; tonight the pub had a point to being here. Most were grouped round the pub door smoking, just one man further up by the narrowboat, staring idly at the vessel.

'*He's* not so smitten!' Ellie said. 'Old Stardust hasn't pulled him.'

Flo frowned as she eyed the man, who had given them the quickest of looks. And another, slower. 'He's either gonna jump in to death by wetness or pull a stroke on that barge.'

Ellie's stomach rolled – but she held her voice steady; she hadn't told Flo about her mother – yet. 'Rob it? You reckon?'

Flo shrugged. 'Dunno. No, not really. He looks too kitted out.'

The man was about the same age as Ellie's father but bigger built, dressed in a dark blue suit with an open-necked shirt where he'd clearly made a late decision to take off his tie and stuff it in his pocket. He had a neat head of receding dark hair and a shiny face as if he'd had a good shave ready for his evening out.

'Don't look!' Ellie said. 'Don't get caught up with him. Definitely looks dodgy to me. Sort who smiles in your face while he's peeing in your handbag!'

Flo shrieked out a laugh that had the man staring at them again, before he walked off along the towpath like someone out with their dog – without the dog. 'You know all the talk, don't you, Chicken?'

'You don't work in a pub without,' Ellie told her.

'Well, if he's not on the blag I reckon he's meeting his girlfriend. Got the look of someone with a bit on the side. Or a reporter...'

'Reporting on what? Ivy Stardust isn't news, she's local history...'

Flo squinted at the canal water, which was just moving, drifting down towards the Basin except where it gushed over the weir on the far side of the lock. 'Perhaps he's gonna report that the Regent's giving short measure, Chicken. In there...'

'What?' Ellie rounded on her new friend. Flo Moses was a great girl to be with, but she wasn't coming any old rubbish like this! 'What are you on about? My dad's never pulled a short pint in his life...'

Flo shrieked again. Good, bad, funny – Flo shrieked, then you waited to be told what she was shrieking for. 'Not you! Ivy Sawdust. She's only half strength, that woman...'

'What do you mean?'

'Them big speakers at the back of the bar. In the alcoves, round from us. They're not connected, are they? She's not quadraphonic, she's two-raphonic...'

Ellie hadn't thought about the entertainers' speakers, they came over loud enough, thank you. 'Must be some fault – why, what are you worried about? You don't reckon her, anyway.'

'Just saying, that's all.' Flo lowered her voice. 'The way they come in, humping all that electrical stuff, roadies with four big speakers, like it was the Docklands Arena. While your dad's not getting what he's paying for, volume-wise...'

'Who's complaining?' But Ellie stared into her friend's face. 'That's the funny thing, though, just between you and me – he doesn't pay her for anything, she sells her own tickets at the door. That's what Rude Boy Wayne Watson's doing at his little table.'

They pulled Pit City faces at one another, and that was it for open-air conversation. A northerly breeze had started whipping off the canal and the girls edged back inside – just as Chris Searle was coming out to the sound of Ivy Stardust winding up with the third chorus of 'Bye-bye Blackbird', the song she'd finished on the week before.

'Hi girls! All right?' he said as he passed them in the doorway, closely followed by an older man who had sat at Ivy Stardust's table and who wheezed and rattled as he walked. 'You're just in time to give Madeleine a hand in the kitchen, cleaning down.'

They nodded, went in to be a bit of help.

'*Madeleine!*' Flo said. 'Not "your friend's mother", not "Mrs. Moses", but *Madeleine*!'

Ellie had never seen bigger eyes. 'Well, it's her name, isn't it? He's just being polite.' She gave Flo a push. 'Don't start anticipating!'

Another shriek. 'Chicken, sometimes what's obvious is...what's obvious!'

The applause broke out for the end of the entertainment and the bar started emptying as Flo danced away through the milling punters to the kitchen, followed by Ellie.

Outside, Chris Searle was being walked along the canal towpath in the direction the man in the suit had gone. The weedy, bald man wheezing next to him had a tight hold of his elbow.

'A word in your ear, guv'nor,' the man was saying, 'then you can get back inside an' cash up.'

'What's on your mind?'

To an onlooker the two of them looked like conspirators, sauntering slowly as the Regent's patrons walked off, up the steps to Salmon Lane or off along the towpath. But the grip remained on Chris's arm.

'Your till won't dis...appoint you, *I* know.' The man coughed up a lungful in the middle of 'disappoint'.

'Don't reckon it will.'

Suddenly, the man stopped. 'Billy Watson,' he said, offering a cold hand to be shaken.

'Yeah, I reckoned, Ivy's...?'

'Worse half. An' this Billy's not best pleased to hear you're thinking of putting the kibosh on her singing nights. Calling it a day.' He jerked his head back towards the pub.

'Am I? Who told you that?'

'A little bird.' Billy Watson gripped Chris's elbow again and resumed the walking, with hardly a glance at the narrowboat that was chugging away northwards.

'Look at that crowd you've 'ad in tonight. Locals, come from all over the manor, all the old flats and streets, everywhere. Very popular, Ivy, bit of a cult figure this way, you prob'ly don't realize, coming from the other side of the river... But not just your locals...'

'Like, further up the canal where that's come from?' Chris asked, nodding at the departing narrowboat. 'Which would be where?'

'Oh, that.' Billy Watson squinted as if he were trying to read the name on her bow.

'Must be some way up there, not to have walked along the towpath...'

'Could be. You can see how Ivy went down: a storm, guv'nor, a storm!'

'Oh, I can see that, Billy. Yeah, I can see that.' Chris pulled his elbow free of Billy Watson's grip and turned to face back towards the Regent's Arms again. 'But to be fair with you, I'm still thinking about my options – and whatever I decide I'll let you know and give good notice.'

Billy Watson lowered his voice. 'Don't go thinking it's the notice.' Which made him cough again. 'I'm not bothered about any notice. I just don't see any sense in putting the tin lid on a good earner...' He kept clearing his throat and wheezing through most of what he said, but it took none of the firmness out of his manner, nor the unblinking cold out of his eyes. 'What you've got to see is, it's in your best interest, an' my best interest, for things to stay as they are.'

Smoke still hung above the door of the pub as the roadie carried out a big speaker single-handed as if it were as light as a stage prop and threw it to another man on board the *Watson Travel* cabin cruiser.

Still looking back, Chris said, 'See, not to talk down your crowd, they weren't any bother, nice people, I'm sure – but I'm dead the rest of the week, and I want to attract a different sort of clientele...'

'I'm sure you've heard the saying about a bird in the hand. Well, what if that bird in the hand is a golden goose? Bit heavy, I know...' Billy Watson chuckled at the expense of a good cough. 'But you sound dangerously like you've made up your mind, guv'nor.' He took Chris's elbow again, turned him, and walked him away from the Regent's Arms.

'No, I said I'm considering my options.'

'Well, I've got something to say to you, to put in your options.' Billy Watson stopped them at a hefty block of concrete that was in the middle of the towpath. 'Which is just to underline for you that a lot of people, *a lot of people,* are gonna be very upset if you call time on Ivy's music nights. An' when I say upset, I mean *really upset.* You think about it.' At which he swore at the concrete block on the towpath, and with enviable ease, suddenly lifted it above his head and threw it well into the canal, one handed.

He turned and stared at Chris. '*Splash!*' he said. He started walking back to the Regent's Arms, coughing. 'Yeah, *splash!*' he repeated, loudly.

here meant freedom from everlasting Mickey Mouse, and the local name for the village was *Le Chat,* which the managers over from America thought was an abbreviation for 'château' but referred to the cat that gave some respite from the mouse. Between shifts, and in the quieter winter months, young people of all nationalities crowded the town's cheap restaurants eating Indian, Chinese and American food – even French, sometimes. It was as cosmopolitan as parts of Paris.

Zlatko Matesa lived in a room above the Café de Montmartre, where most of the local smoking, drinking and gambling went on. The bar was busy from early morning till late at night as shifts at Disneyland came off and went on, with Zlatko Matesa coming and going irregularly like someone covering other peoples' stints, his sleeps as short as Frederic the bar owner's, but much less predictable.

It was hard to tell where Zlatko Matesa came from because nobody really knew him. 'East European' was an odds-on bet, perhaps a Balkans man, in his mid-thirties. He drank alone and he ate alone, and the only time he was to be seen with others was when he arrived with a minibus of young people from the Disneyland direction, and dropped them off at a rooming house up a side street beyond the old marketplace, acting like a foreman of some sort. Disneyland people came and went, but the goings in the mornings were mostly before the locals were up. The local understanding, though, was that these youngish workers who came and went with the man in the minibus were dressed up all day as seven dwarves, or Donald Duck's cousins, or Sinbad's thieves. But however loudly they performed at work, here in Château Renoir-sur-Marne they kept themselves to themselves, and hardly uttered a word in any language that anybody heard.

This evening the bar at the Café de Montmartre was busy as usual. As the new guv'nor of the Regent's Arms in Limehouse might be sitting following the patterns on the wallpaper, *le patron* here hardly paused between serving drinks, slapping little plastic mats and wet bills onto tables, and reaching over for the next order. Zlatko Matesa sat at the back of the narrow bar, surrounded by the space everyone seemed to want to leave him. His drink was a poisonous-looking green, his cigarette the most acrid in the place, and his expression outdid both. He sat, smoked and drank, and scowled at his mobile phone until it finally obeyed him, and rang. He refused to snap it open immediately, but only after a long drag at his cigarette, as if he knew that no one dared not give him time to answer.

And then nobody in the bar knew what he said into it, because none of them understood: but after finishing his drink – and smoking another cigarette, slowly – he got up and left the bar. And despite the bar being close-packed and busy, it was a good ten minutes – and after the table was wiped – before a couple of Disneyland Cinderella lookalike girls moved from standing in a corner to come over and sit there.

For Ellie it wasn't all hand-in-hand with Flo. She didn't even know where her new friend lived, except that from school it was in the opposite direction to the Regent's Arms. Flo headed off to 'the flat', not 'the house', and there were a couple of tower blocks visible from the second floor of the school, so perhaps Ellie could see where Flo lived without knowing it. But for some reason she didn't like to ask; Flo hadn't offered any more information about herself, and Ellie didn't want to seem nosy; plus her first priority was to get to know her own patch.

From the Regent there was the choice to go off into one sort of East London or into a different one altogether. Limehouse Basin and the Thames was the direction Ellie's dad wanted to face, where his upmarket clientele would come from. Ellie's real preference would be the same direction but to go further on across the river and back to the south side of the Thames. That was where her heart still lay; that was her home; because her home would always be the place where her mother had died. The other direction, inland away from the river, that was unknown territory, Ivy Stardust's queendom, what the singer reckoned was her old, proud, dyed-in-the-wool East End, all around the Mile End Road. Except that everything had changed over the past thirty years, the little local shops were Asian and African street markets now; and there were so many modern blocks of flats in Tower Hamlets that there weren't many streets of houses left. Everything changes whether people seek it or not; but, most of all, Ellie's life had changed.

Ellie would never forget the afternoon it happened. She was just in from school, the pub was quiet and her mother had gone up to have her bath, well before the Cherry Tree's evening opening. She always did the lunch-hour bar duty, and then Ellie's dad would take over, having had his 'five minutes'' kip on the settee. Everything was quiet: too quiet, as Ellie remembered it later, going to her bedroom with her school bag, past the bathroom door. She had got on with her homework – she liked to get school stuff out of the way – and time had passed until she was wondering whether to make a cup of tea or get another Coke. She remembered her dad calling up the stairs to her mum, wanting to know where the Lucky Seven tickets were, and getting no reply. He'd given it a few minutes and he'd called up again. And then again, louder. There was still no reply. And the next Ellie heard was her father coming up the stairs and thumping on the bathroom door. Thumping and thumping and calling her mother's name. 'Jen! Jenny! You all right in there?'

By now Ellie was out of her bedroom and standing behind her father on the landing. 'Mum! Mum! Say something!'

And her father had suddenly put his shoulder to the bathroom door and charged it in.

Ellie would never forget the animal sound her father made, the primal cry of despair. He slammed the bathroom door shut to prevent Ellie from seeing what he had seen, and all she heard was her father shouting her mother's name and the overflowing slosh of water on the floor. Ellie screamed – and in seconds one of the regulars from the bar was up there with them, barging past her into the bathroom – and coming straight out to lead her away from the scene.

Her father had found her mother in the bath under the water, lying there like Snow White in her glass coffin, he said, looking up as if any second she was going to rise up out of the water and talk. She still looked beautiful, the bruise where she'd hit as she slipped was on the back of her head; and there was no blood, no terrible gory mess. And Ellie could see the scene; still life; a still death, accidental — by drowning when unconscious. She could only picture it, but it was vivid in her head, and every time she looked at a photo of her mother she had to wave away the imaginary water that she saw covering her face.

And now they had only come to live by a canal! By a lock and a weir, where water was a background sound to everything...

Since her mother had died Ellie had taken to walking a lot, on her own. She traipsed many streets, and asked many questions in her head — some questions so big that no person on earth knew the answers, not for sure. And now the nearest place to walk was by the canal, along the dog-mucked and spat-upon towpath, those first gloomy metres of waterway en route to the Midlands, where the only sign of movement most days was the Canary Wharf office joggers in their lunch hours, and the dog owners. But Ellie forced herself to walk by the water, because only by overcoming her fear of drowning could she really start to move on.

After school one afternoon, facing south towards the river, she made herself take a careful look at the Basin — the yachts, the narrowboats, the small cruisers; and, overlooking them, the smart apartments all around, some of them designed to look like the prows of ships — and whose prices in the estate agents' windows made light of a few noughts. Yes, she thought, her dad's upmarket restaurant scheme could definitely pay off around here. Which for him was good, but for her a secret disappointment, because he might succeed big time and they'd be stuck this side of the river for ever.

But in her heart she knew that sort of thinking was just stupid. You never go back anywhere in life except carrying flowers, and Ellie always tried like mad not to stare any way but into the light. So it was get on with it – deal with her fear of water, help her dad, see which way he ended up going, and go with him. In the meantime there was homework to do, school to go to, Rude Boy Watson to give a big miss, and Flo to get to know better: so all Ellie's walks soon led back to the Regent's Arms.

Fang Song Yin suddenly didn't want to go. Village people talked glibly about the young ones in the region leaving home as if they were going off on short visits somewhere, but this was no trip to a cousin in Hanyang that Song was taking – it was a life-changing journey to the other side of the world. Her mother wasn't old, but she coughed a lot, and quickly ran out of breath – and Song lay awake with the dreadful thought that she might never see her alive again. Which was made worse by her mother being so brave. Why couldn't she cry, beg her not to go, wail about her own loneliness? Perhaps, then, Song might have changed her mind, stayed, and hoped for better things. But, no, her mother walked about the place as if she weren't a little stooped, stifled her coughing into a cloth, and always looked at Song with clear, dry eyes.

'You've got to go, child. Your father is looking down and willing you to go. I am a peasant, but you have your talent, and you have some education. Farming the fields is not for you – and if the crops improve, I will get a boy to help. Go! You have to chase your destiny, for us all.'

But Song knew that this was bravado, the act of a loving mother for her only daughter; she had caught glimpses of the anguish in her mother's eyes. But she had also seen in her daydreams the face of her father, smiling and crying at the same time as she sang for him, as he clapped his hands in rhythm to her melody. He had done it right from when she was a little girl till the week he died. 'You are special, little daughter, you are special.'

For the past few days Song had said nothing more about going. She had packed her rucksack, and cleaned her room, put flowers in a vase on her table to give a few days' fragrance after she had left it, and been more loving to her mother than she'd ever been. This following of her destiny was the only way, though, she kept telling herself: when she was successful – even just a little – money would soon be coming back from the organizers. Money for

Uncle Chen's payments, and also money for her mother, to bring some proper comfort to her life.

And now Song had to do the going, and it was hard, hard. With the truck waiting and its driver hooting, the feel of this final hug at the gate had to be remembered for a very long time. But it had to be done quickly. Her departure had to be just as if she was only going off to Hanyang – and with no looking back.

'Write to me,' her mother said. 'I've got good eyes for reading.'

'As soon as I get there.'

'Goodbye, then, Song.' Her mother stood back, with the most fragile smile on her lips, her eyes shining. 'Be good!'

'I will. Goodbye, Mother.' Song threw her rucksack up into the back of the open truck, where another girl and a young man were watching, perhaps thinking of their own farewells. Song climbed up after it, with just time to get a grip on the side before the truck pulled impatiently away. She resolutely made herself look out along the road to the front, not wanting to see her mother waving goodbye, to see no last image of childhood to weep over; and it was a kilometre before she turned to exchange names with the others.

Hsaio-Yueh Lin, the girl, and Lao Zi had come from a town to the south where Uncle Chen also had a shady *spot, all three on the same journey – to a better life. And this was the first leg, the truck to take them north to Nanjing, where they would sleep the night and receive their travelling papers.*

The road was narrow but in fair condition, and as the day wore on and the others dozed under a warm sun, Fang Song Yin pulled a small, cheap notebook from her shirt and started to write; the start of her first letter back to her mother. She was bright and cheerful, and wrote of the trees in blossom along the way, and the birds that she had heard singing; although in her heart she knew how difficult her journey would be. But she knew also that the spirits of her father and her mother would smile on her like constant stars.

She read her letter through when it was finished, and tucked the notebook back into her shirt, and finally cried, and cried.

'That's stupid!' Lao Zi's voice brought her back to the bump of the truck. Song realized that his eyes hadn't been closed all the time. 'It's over, the past. You look back too much and you twist your head off like a dead chicken.'

Fang Song Yin looked at him. He was leaning on an elbow, stretched out, languid, despite the rattle of the road. 'A philosopher!' she said, making the word sound as if it tasted of a bitter fruit.

'A realist,' he replied. 'You should throw away your sad little book and concentrate on what is to come.' And he smiled as he went on staring at her.

Ellie and her dad did go back south of the river, for one purpose – to go to the cash 'n' carry where Chris Searle bought most stuff except his drinks. Drinks, printed bar towels and beer mats came by brewery delivery, but everything else – glasses, plates, crisps and peanuts, pork scratchings, cigarettes, tea cloths, and most of what Ellie and her father ate – came from the cash 'n' carry on the Thames Barrier industrial estate. With a long cart they worked their way down the wide aisles hoisting off shelves, arguing as usual over quantities, with Ellie, as usual, winning. Well, she did the books...

And at a crucial moment in one of the aisles, in the act of clutching at a caterers' pack of paper napkins – not heavy, but slippery in its shrink wrap – Ellie met the boy, coming the other way. With the pack squeezed in her arms, it jumped like a huge bar of wet soap out of her grip and hit him on the leg.

'Thanks a lot!'

'Sorry...'

Not Rude Boy, but a boy in her form, good-looking with black, shiny gel-spiked hair, clear dark skin, brown eyes, and white teeth in a nice smile – where most at Limehouse High had their mouths knotted in sneers. It was Jasbinder Prabhaker. Jaz, from their class, the boy who used to sit next to Flo.

'New girl!'

'It jumped! Life of its own!' Ellie looked round to where her dad had gone on pulling the long cart, engrossed by the differences in two fat rolls of cling film.

'What you doing over here?' The boy made her presence sound the greatest of pleasures as he gave her back the paper napkins.

Her first thought was to tell him to mind his own business; but something about him decided Ellie to be pleasanter than that. 'We run a pub, the Regent's Arms, on the canal...'

'Ah.'

'What about you?' He seemed to be on his own.

'We've got a trade card. Telly for the bedroom, those Asian channels for my mum.' He pulled a face. 'On offer this month...'

Ellie made a show of looking around. There was no one with Jaz, and this wasn't even the electrical section.

'...And she wants some kitchen foil. You seen any?'

'Shelf there's *foil* of it.' She jerked her head. He gave her a bad-joke smile as she followed up quickly. 'On the left.'

He saw it. 'Yeah. Cheers.' He picked the biggest — eighty metres of turkey-sized aluminium. 'Good to see you, Ellie.'

'And you.' *Ellie!* So he knew her name! There was a little spurt in Ellie's inside, one of those thrill things like at a fairground. But not all pleasant, it was one of those mixed-up feelings — because with his name came his reputation, his reputation with Flo. He was the boy who couldn't keep his hands to himself, currently out in the cold till he learned better manners and Flo whistled him back — which wouldn't be long, going by the way she'd called him dishy... And which was neither here nor there, except that in a stupid, instant sort of way, Ellie quite liked him.

The Regent's Arms was quiet — Saturday-through-to-Thursday quiet — with even less evening trade than it did in the middle of the day. Back from the cash 'n' carry, Ellie was upstairs at her homework, while Chris was in the bar having a meeting, by arrangement.

It was with a woman, Dot Bartram, one of their local councillors. Chris had found her details at the town hall and invited her in for a drink. Like Ivy Stardust, she drank Baileys, but she had made sure that she paid for it; she was not the sort to be corrupted. In her fifties, with dyed blonde hair up in a coil, she was no stranger to a slice of cake – as Chris would put it. In fact, she was big, with the dainty eating fingers of a weight-watcher as she allowed herself to be just a bit corrupted by the free crisps in the bowl on the table.

'What was it you wanted to know?' she asked, with a straight official edge to her voice. 'I'm a councillor, you appreciate, not an officer...'

'Sure, but you're on the Planning Committee...'

'The Chair.'

'...And I'm new here, you're one of my ward councillors, so I thought it'd be good to meet. A new landlord can always use all the local information going...'

'But, specifically...?' Councillor Cake had a cautious, tapped-telephone voice. 'You said you're seeking some change of use?'

'Well, don't I need to?' Chris waved an arm in the empty air. 'Seven in the evening? This place is dead on its feet!'

'That's the previous landlord.' Another cheeky little crisp tempted the councillor. 'He let it all go downhill, except for Friday nights...'

'Sure. Ivy Stardust. I'd be on the dole if it wasn't for her.' The new guv'nor poured the councillor another Baileys from the bottle he'd left handy on the table, raised a 'no' finger at her as she reached for her purse. 'That's the other half of what you paid for.'

Dot Bartram nodded like a committee chair allowing a point of order. 'Used to be big in local business, Ivy Watson,' she said as she sipped.

'Anyhow—'

'Very successful with her coaches, but trade's dropped off against the big national companies...'

'Got a good voice, though.' Chris Searle knew when to go along with the referee.

Dot Bartram nodded, and she was going to say something else but she didn't, as if she were leaving Chris an opening to make his pitch.

'Well, this plan...' he said. 'As you know, the publican's trade is nothing like it was. TV, cheap drinks in Asda – beer sells in here like snow in Eskimo-land...'

'Would that be Greenland or Alaska...?'

'Just a saying.' He'd made a politically incorrect mistake, but went on anyway. 'No one much sits around in a pub and drinks pints any more, that's what I mean.'

The councillor had to agree. Her neck folded and flapped as she nodded her head; she was the only person Chris Searle had met who made a noise, nodding. 'Licensed premises are dying as public houses,' she said. 'So they change their names, turn themselves into carveries, let the under-age juveniles in, and still they find life hard...'

Now it was the guv'nor nodding. She was telling him!

'...And that's because there's no community any more.' Dot Bartam spoke in concise you-can-quote-me-on-this mode. 'Thatcher told us there's no such thing as society: well, I'm here to say that there is: but *community*, that's another matter. There's your community, if we don't do something about it.' She swung round to point at the Sky television set as if Chris Searle's Hitachi were to blame for all the local ills. 'No contact, no brotherhood, no sisterhood.' She sipped at her glass of Baileys like it was rostrum water at a council meeting and she was the speaker holding forth.

'So what I want to do is different from any of that.' Chris jumped in. 'Limehouse Basin,' he said, 'the posh apartments, they're the ones I want to attract; offer them their lunch and their dinner.' He waved his hand towards the open door, and the towpath. 'Upgrade the whole place this side of the Basin. It's a vision I've got – a smart canal-side venue with an Italian menu...'

But he had wrong-footed again. This wasn't the direction in which the councillor wanted to see her ward going.

'What? Serving crate-reared veal, calves' liver, somewhere exclusively for the "haves" – who lord it here in their superior apartments putting nothing back into the area...?'

'I dunno. They pay their council tax. And I'll take on more staff, local people, that's what you're after, isn't it? Jobs.'

Dot Bartram didn't shake her head, didn't nod, simply stared straight at him. 'In my humble opinion you should be looking the other way, landlord: Stepney Way, the High Street, the Ocean Estate, round there. Look to them. Do something for the real locals – as well as giving them their local entertainment. Affordable fish and chip suppers in a nice setting; not forgetting the Indians, somewhere away from the traffic; or cater to the Afro-Caribbean trade, they're under-represented in restaurants; all these people who belong here now.' She was still sitting, but clearly about to get up: and her opinion was far from humble, majority-party councillors' opinions never were.

'Or Chinese takeaways?' Chris asked.

'Well, they're local, those who stayed. The Chinese have been around here for two hundred years. You could definitely think about that. Cater for the majority, not the rich few. Your "haves" have got it all already, we don't need to put more white wine sauce on *their* plates.' Now she did get up.

Chris Searle got up with her. 'Well, okay, but do you reckon I need to extend my catering licence to upgrade from bar snacks – and what about planning if my kitchen stays within the building as is...? That's the sort of thing I need to know, whether it's for fish and chips or chicken tikka masala.'

Dot Bartram stared at him importantly, powerfully; local politicians held more sway than the prime minister where community life went. 'Oh, no doubt you'll need all that. Go to one of my officers at the town hall. Give my name if you like; say I've advised you to seek information. But you remember what I said...' She was ready to go, shoulder bag slung across her front. 'Before you put in an application, you think hard about what we really need around here. Meanwhile, you could do a lot worse than Ivy Stardust.'

And she went – with one thing very certain; Councillor Cake definitely carried some weight around there.

CHAPTER FIVE

As a publican's daughter, Ellie could spot trouble well before it started: such as two men who wouldn't look at one another; the first raising of a woman's voice; or the landing of a hand a smack too loud on a table. Early signs of the 'all-off'. And Ellie could see Rude Boy's stare across the Limehouse High School yard the second she came through the gate, a daggers look that surely meant trouble. She knew it was serious because instead of waggling his tongue disgustingly at her, he immediately looked away as if his head had been jerked by a wire. Something was coming, and it wouldn't be long before it did, Ellie knew that.

'Chicken!'

And here came trouble of a different sort, weaving through a juggle of footballing boys. Ellie could just hear the rant that Flo would go into if she knew about Ellie and Jaz Prabhaker having a chat in the cash 'n' carry. Okay, she'd know that it had to have been an accident, but that wouldn't stand in the way of a good mouthful of contempt for the boy she was hanging out to dry. Why open that furnace door? So Ellie had already decided to keep her mouth shut: but at the last minute she asked herself, could that be a mistake, if Flo found out later? *'Why didn't you tell me about it if it was so flamin' innocent? Eh, Goldilocks?'* Yes, there was always that danger, and Flo was always only a glint away from danger. But Jaz Prabhaker had nothing to show off about, picking up a packet of serviettes that had fallen his way, so he wouldn't crow, and Ellie wouldn't, either. She firmed up. It was better to keep quiet about it and say, 'Oh, *him*?' if anything soaked through; after all, it wasn't as if they'd had a snog in the catering aisle, was it?

'Hiya, Flo! How you doin', girl?' Ellie could turn on a twinkle like Ivy Stardust herself.

'Shouldn't have ate that breakfast. So, what's new?'

'Only Rude Boy over there. He's giving me the dead eyeball.'

'Oh, stick him, Chicken. But have I got a buzz for you! Oh, yeah! Or, you heard, have you?' Flo stared into Ellie's eyes, her own wide enough to promise a world exclusive any second. 'You been told?'

Ellie shook her head. 'What about?' *About school? One of the teachers?* But she wasn't going to know what it was just yet. The football that had been bouncing high and hard took a skid off a miskick and suddenly whacked into the back of Flo's head – and no one ever saw the football posse run away so fast.

Which was followed by the bell, and registration, and morning assembly, and all at once it was, 'See you at break, Chicken...' because Flo and Ellie split into their different sets for maths. 'Tell you then!'

But at break time – as if he well knew his short opportunity to get Ellie on her own – Rude Boy suddenly blew his nasty breath into her face. She was heading across the small quadrangle between the Art Room and the Drama Studio, making for her meeting with Flo by the dining hall snack machine, when out he stepped from behind the colonnade like some villain in a Shakespeare play.

'Well. Ellie skin-an'-bone Searle!' he said.

'What? Dog's-breath? Get out of my way!'

He didn't. He grabbed hard at Ellie's arm. 'Don' give me that guv'nor's daughter's grief! When Wayne Watson wants a word with anyone this side of the water, he has it...' He yanked her into him.

'An' what Wayne Watson will have – either side of the water – is a knee in the nuts if he doesn't let go my arm!' Ellie jerked her arm away, because she meant it; she had never been one for empty words, they were never worth the exercising of the mouth muscles.

But straight off, Rude Boy grabbed her again, the other arm this time. 'You listen to me!' He pushed his face into hers and she smelled last night's curry. 'You make sure your poxy dad knows a good thing when he's got one goin'! Right? Him an' his *options*!' And now Ellie knew that her dad had to have let something out. 'Just a friendly word of advice...'

It felt far from friendly. He still had a grab on Ellie's arm, and while his face was still thrust into hers, as good as her word but giving nothing away by a change in her expression, she suddenly brought her knee up hard into Wayne Watson's groin. Action – reaction.

'Oomph!' he said, taking it badly.

'An' a friendly word to you. I politely requested you to let go my arm,' Ellie told him coldly, 'so next time, let go!' as the kid made a desperate attempt to look as if nothing was hurting – but suddenly spared one hand from his groin to lift his arm to slap her.

But no blow landed. Because Wayne Watson's swiping arm was suddenly blocked by someone else's – by Jaz Prabhaker's as he came past, hefting his slipping school bag back up onto his shoulder.

'Oop! Sorry,Wayne, mate! That your arm?' Somehow he made it look and sound as if it really had been an accidental block.

'Get out of it, scum!' But the moment had gone, a crowd of others came through, and Wayne Watson went off, walking as normally as he could manage. 'You remember!' he shouted over his shoulder at Ellie. 'What I said.' But he went away coughing and wheezing like his father.

Jaz Prabhaker still had the look of innocence on him.

'I can fight my own battles, thank you! Leave it out!' Ellie told him.

The boy shrugged, and walked off. But Ellie, looking after him, was not nearly as annoyed as she'd made it sound. That had been a bit brave, she had to say: above and beyond the call of duty, because Wayne Watson was a bad enemy to have.

But what would her dad think to what Rude Boy had said, if she told him? Why was so much aggro going on over a grotty little pub in East London? Ellie had to wonder if her dad wasn't getting in over his head. And she churned in her stomach at her unhappy choice of metaphor.

Mrs. I. Watson, Director, sat at her desk on a comfortable leather chair; so comfortable that it had been patched, and patched again, with strips of carpet-joining tape. Like any performer offstage, she looked very different from the Ivy Stardust of Friday nights. But not drabber like the chair; she was smart, the businesswoman, a sort of older sister of Stardust with her hair streaked grey. She was taking a phone call, the cracked and frosted glass door to the outer office closed: no one ever came in here, Mrs. Watson went out to see people.

She was listening, no nods, no 'yeses' or 'uh-huhs', it could have been a recorded message at the other end — until suddenly she said, 'Hold on,' and got up to look at a big chart on the wall. It was a calendar, with blocks of different colours going across one day here, two days there, three days, a week — the commitments of her coaches.

'Wednesday,' she said, 'next week, the twenty-sixth.' Her facial expression didn't change as she switched into French, with an East End accent. '*Vingt-six.*' Then, '*Armentières, comme d'habitude.*' And she clicked off the phone, to mark a 'P' on the coloured-in block covering

24th, 25th, 26th September, which already had *World War I* written along it.

She lit a cigarette, said something through the smoke, blew out, and took her mobile phone from her street-market 'Gucci' handbag. It was a long time answering; then, 'Billy?' she asked. 'We need euros for next week. Plus, I've had someone from Dot Bartram's office on, first thing, tipped me the wink. Our man's still got plans.' Billy said something. 'I think push might have to come to shove, boy. Your little word done *no* good.' And she stared into space, with a face as hard as grinding stone, inhaling on her cigarette as if it were an oxygen lifeline.

'I've just mashed Rude Boy's potatoes,' Ellie reported to Flo. Which had to be translated – talking to a cook's daughter! – and when it was, it brought a great whoop from the girl.

'Hurt his pride, then!'

Ellie's voice was deep in her throat with indignation. 'He was coming on about my poxy dad – his word – knowing a good thing when he saw one. It's like protection, the old racket. You give 'em what they want, and they make sure your pub doesn't burn down. Or something. Entertainment tax, they used to call it.'

'That's criminal!' Flo said. 'But they can't take *that*

much money on the door. Not worth threatening for, is it...?'

'I don't know; perhaps it's *her*, doing her thing. Having her public...' Ellie shrugged. 'But why does it have to be in my dad's pub.'

There was a short silence. 'So we'll see what happens Friday night.' Flo gave Ellie a look as she said it. Words sometimes carry more than their meanings, and the eyes tell you when.

'You're coming again on Friday, then?' Ellie asked. 'You got nothing better to do, girl?'

'Nothing,' Flo replied. 'An' that's my bit of news I was telling you...'

And Ellie didn't know why, but her stomach started to roll. Something told her that Flo's bit of news wasn't going to be the signal for buying a box of Celebrations. Really good news you didn't have to wait half the morning to hear.

Flo put an arm around Ellie. 'He's asked my mum out...'

'Who? Rude Boy?' But Ellie knew it wasn't, of course, it wasn't even a funny joke – but if she hadn't *said* something her mouth would have made some stupid sound, because she knew who Flo meant all right.

'Your dad. Rang her up last night and asked her out...'

'He can't go out,' Ellie protested. 'He's stuck in a pub...'

Flo put her head on one side. 'Ain't you pleased, Chicken?'

'Yeah, of course I'm pleased, I'm just, not quite understanding...' But Ellie's smile wouldn't have fooled a two-year-old.

'What, then?'

'When and where – and why didn't he tell me? He *tells* me important stuff, always has...' Ellie heard herself carping instead of celebrating.

'You're saying he doesn't reckon this is important?'

'No, I...'

'I know – *more*, he reckons it's *too* important. Yeah, him telling you wouldn't be just a crackle with the cornflakes, would it, it ain't that sort of news. He's got to think about it, lay it on a bit delicate...'

'Like you have?'

'No, you know me, Chicken...'

Yes, Ellie thought, about as closely as I want to for now; friend was fine, sister, no. But she didn't say it. Just, 'Whatever...' was what she got out as the bell went for double English.

She gave him a good row when she got in from school. He was seeing in a delivery of Danish lager in kegs, down the awkward steps – although already he had created a slide with a turn in it, each keg landing with a thump and a bounce on the thick rope mat at the bottom. Which was nothing to the thump Ellie wanted to give to him when the dockets had been signed.

'You got something to tell me?' she asked him.

And he knew – of course he knew, Ellie thought – his open mouth and no words coming out said that he knew. Standing there, guilt all over him like a cold shower, he'd had all day to think about it, probably all last night as well, and still he didn't have a word in his head for her.

'Flo Moses' mum – have you asked her out?'

'Asked her out?'

'Are you deaf? Asked her out – as in "asked her out"! Picked up the phone when I was well asleep and said, "Madeleine Moses, will you go out with me?" *Asked her out!*'

'Oh, that "asked her out"...'

Ellie would have smacked her hand down hard on the bar, but that would have hurt. So she just stared.

'Not the way you think, Ellie.' His voice came out high and reedy, like pleading with a referee not to book him. 'If I'm going to put in a proper application to the council I'm going to have to know my needs kitchen-wise. Mrs. Moses, Flo's mother...'

'Madeleine. Say it.'

'Madeleine – I'm not embarrassed to say it, Lady Jane

– she'll know the size of my fridge. I'm picking her brain, that's all, Ellie. There's nothing else to it...'

'Well if there was anything else, I'd hope you'd tell me, before I have to get it off the woman's daughter.' Ellie stood back off him and looked up into his face. 'But don't, eh? Not too quick. I'm not ready for it, Dad, I'm not over...' Her voice tailed off as she stared down at the floor.

Her father nodded. But people nod when they don't want to definitely commit themselves. You can't read out a nod as evidence in court, you can't throw a nod back in someone's face. And when Ellie went to bed – having learned that the meeting would be the next Tuesday afternoon when Annie was looking after the pub – she didn't sleep for a very long time. The lager in the kegs that had bounced down the slide settled long before Ellie Searle could.

Song felt sick with tiredness. It was a long way to Nanjing on the back of a small truck, now her rucksack of soft clothes had become a bag of stones after the thousandth bump on the bad road. It was late at night, and they were driving through a poor touristy quarter of the city, with erratic flashing lights, loud music, sudden shouts, and the smell of cheap fast food. Girls and boys hung about in dingy doorways, and fat men like Uncle Chen sat at rickety tables outside sordid bars. Song wanted the truck to get quickly through this district to somewhere pleasanter: but the streets only grew narrower and narrower, and they had to stop by a foul-smelling open drain. The driver slammed his cab door and shouted at the three of them, 'Come on! Get off! Follow me!'

Song looked about fearfully at the toothless faces and the leering eyes, asking herself if this was what she and her mother were in debt for – trudging through this squalor? But as she picked her way through the filthy alleys she tried to hold her head up high, she was a singer, she was on her way to fulfil her ambition to lift people with her voice: she had to be way above the gutter.

The truck driver took them to a small, old-fashioned house with a curling roof – to be met at the doorway by a well-dressed woman, who looked to Song as if she belonged in a much grander neighbourhood. She was older than Song's mother, with her hair top-knotted in traditional-style, and as carefully made-up as an actress; a slim and silky woman – with a voice like the growl of a guard dog.

'You're late – and you brought the truck too close! Stupid!' She looked as if she might have slapped the truck driver round the head had he not been standing too far back. 'You! In there!' She pushed the young man, Lao Zi, into the first room, where Song caught a glimpse of other men unrolling sleeping bags. She stepped back, so as not to be pushed herself by this woman.

'What's the matter with you?' the woman sneered. 'You want to go back to your village?' But there was a look in her eyes that warned against doing that, much as Song might like to, right now. This was all backstreet stuff, and already Song knew too much for her own good about where she was, and how she had got there. 'Give me your money!' the woman snapped, clicking her fingers at both the new girls – while a big man who looked like a weightlifter came down the stairs and went into the men's room, closing the door behind him. A sardonic laugh from Lao Zi was immediately stifled. So much for the philosopher!

Song had never felt so much at the mercy of other people. She had signed her name on Uncle Chen's paper, so she didn't even own herself any more. She rooted into her rucksack and found the envelope given to her under the magnolia tree. She offered it slowly – for it to be taken with a snatch.

'If it's not all here there'll be trouble!'

'It's not money. It's a note from Uncle Chen.'

The woman twisted her mouth at the name. She read the note, and turned her cold eyes on Song. 'You'd better be worth the chance he takes!' she growled.

Ellie couldn't be sure when the plan first came to her. She didn't wake up with it running off across her pillow, it wasn't born on a dream; those sorts of plans become nonsense in reality. What seems feasible in sleep turns ridiculous once you're awake. This plan just grew; it simply became what Ellie was going to do, something for her mother's memory – not yet dead a year – just a vague idea at first but starting to run through her blood. Meanwhile, another music night came and went. With Flo. And with Flo's mother operating big time in the kitchen.

Ellie wasn't in the bar waiting for them this Friday night. She watched them come along Salmon Lane from her bedroom at the back, Flo and her mother clicking down the steps from the road; nor was she there to be faced with Rude Boy when he arrived. Wayne Watson had ignored Ellie during the rest of the week in school, and he ignored her tonight. But that Friday night Ellie especially didn't want to see what looks went on between her dad and Flo's mother; because from Cherry Tree customers she knew all the flirty looks going – the not-particularly-looking-at-each-other look, which would have told her the worst news; or the long stare across a crowded room, straight out of a slushy film; or the eye-to-eye-slow-blink, which would still be saying much too much. Ellie would really rather not know, thanks.

She gave it three or four minutes, then down she came,

carrying a box of the paper serviettes that she'd deliberately taken upstairs *to* bring down. All as matter-of-fact and as businesslike as the music that was setting up.

'Chicken!'

'Flo!'

'Where you been?'

'Fetching these.' Ellie put the serviettes on the table, into the aroma of Flo's mother's perfume – expensive, subtle, and with a slight provocative edge, a sort of scarlet musk. And her make-up must have taken an hour because Madeleine Moses looked gorgeous – and didn't it just fit that Ellie's dad was in his best, favourite James Bond blue linen shirt, two neck buttons undone? The dog! Ivy Stardust was well upstaged tonight; it was a good job Flo's mother was in the kitchen out of the general view, or there might have a sulk from the stage. As it was, the music night was very standard, no highs, no lows – but as busy as ever, in the same sorts of ways as before, and not a look to suggest the threatening that Ellie had taken from Rude Boy.

'I've got burger rolls today, you start slicing them –' Flo's mother told Ellie – 'an' you stick these burgers in the fridge,' – to Flo, as she pulled four unmarked catering packs of burgers from her freezer bag.

Ellie didn't know why she felt so lumpy seeing Flo and her mother treating the fridge like their own – after all, this was all to help her dad make a go of the night, all extra profit ringing into the till — but she felt elbowed, even physically, onto a side table as the other two moved about in her kitchen. She was so out of sorts that she nearly gave someone a slice of finger in their snack, except that the first knife she'd picked up wasn't sharp enough.

'That's not the knife for the job,' Flo's mother told her, smiling like a supervisor with a work-experience girl. 'We cut 'em, Baby, not rough 'em up...' She passed the right sharp tool over to Ellie.

Who took it without a word, but with a sinister thought.

Like the week before, the girls got out of the thick atmosphere when they could. Ivy Stardust — in gold tonight — gave the customers what they wanted, but it was the same old repertoire, just varied in its order.

Flo spotted a difference, though. 'Tell you who's not here tonight,' she said, as if by way of conversation.

Ellie could think of someone special who wasn't there tonight, but, sadly, who never would be. 'Who's that?'

'Those men. Sitting at that main table last week. Gangster-looking, spooky, cold like snakes...' She shivered her shoulders, for effect.

Ellie hadn't noticed the audience tonight, she'd had her mind on what Flo's reaction was going to be to her secret plan. But she remembered the men well enough, some foreign-sounding, one Liverpool, they'd given her the shivers, too; there's a chill people like that gave off that goes inside to the bones. 'Probably robbing a bank,' she tried to joke.

'Eating babies!' And they both went '*Uuuggh!*'

Outside, during the main break, walking the towpath with customers who were smoking and chatting, Flo asked the question.

'You all right, Chicken?'

'Yeah. Sure.' Which was a lie; otherwise, why was she concocting a plan?

'You're not acting like it...'

Ellie shrugged; she'd only ever told Flo the bare bones of what had happened, and now definitely wasn't the time to bring mothers into things. And she didn't have to, because there, along the towpath, was the solitary man they'd seen the previous Friday.

'None of those long boats here tonight, neither,' Flo whispered, noticing what Ellie hadn't, 'so he's definitely after something else...'

And Ellie didn't like what that might be – he was staring through the windows of the Regent's Arms right now – although this time he didn't wander off when he saw them there, he came over towards them, dressed more casually than before – a Nike shirt and a black sweater slung over his shoulders, Italian-style, not really going well with a body built as big as his.

'Bit old for you?' he asked, a jerk of his head towards the public house, eyes centred on the pair of them, though.

'What?' Did he think they were under-age drinkers? Was he from the council, one of Councillor Cake's officers? The cheek of it! Ellie was the landlord's daughter.

'That music...'

'Can you hear it all right out here?' she asked. Or was he one of those mean devils who wouldn't pay at the door or buy a drink?

'Enough. I'm very fond of Ella Fitzgerald and Frank Sinatra; prefer Judy – but Ivy's not got the Garland magic...' He had put his hands in his pockets, very casual now, and looking the more suspicious for that as he took the two of them in. 'Can't stand the smoke around the door, though. You only get one set of lungs...'

'I like some of that stuff, as it goes – we always have 'em playing on the jukebox,' Ellie told the man. 'This is my dad's place...'

'I know, love,' he said – before, hands still in his pockets, he strolled casually on down towards Limehouse Basin.

Ellie frowned. 'How the hell does he know that?' she asked Flo when the man couldn't hear, passing the gushing water by the lock gate.

'Perhaps he's a prowler,' Flo said darkly, 'so keep your curtains drawn...'

At which they pulled faces at one another, and Ellie thought how great it would be if Flo could just be a really good mate – with no chance of being a stepsister, and no need for her plan...

Inside, later, when the music had finished, Flo nodded at what she'd noticed before – the mute speaker, one of the bigger pair being carried out single-handed. 'See that?' she asked. 'You see that come in?'

'Yeah, I think so.'

'Well, run the video, watch it again...'

Ellie tried to look back; but she wasn't the old Ellie tonight: like that first knife in the kitchen, she wasn't too sharp. 'No, it's gone,' she said. 'Why? What's the big deal?'

'The big deal, my girl, is that it took two musclemen to bring it in...'

'Yeah...'

'...An' only one to carry it out.'

Ellie frowned, tried to see the significance.

'An' does it give out any sound?' Flo let it sink in. 'Don't know about tonight, but not last week, it didn't.' She looked at Ellie with eyes like headlights, main beam. 'It's a fake. I reckon it's a fake with something in it when it comes in, and nothing in it when it goes out...'

Ellie stared back — while the other speaker went out, also one-handed.

'Plus you've got prowler matey turning up again outside, eyes everywhere but not coming in, and those gorillas from gangland don't show up...' Ellie shivered. Flo could make anything sound as scary as a horror film. 'Something's going on, Chicken, something weird's going on around here...'

But before either of them could dwell on that, it was time for Flo to go. Coming round from the bar Ellie's dad was making a show of paying Flo's mother for her kitchen services — with an envelope already marked 'M' — not 'M.M.' or 'M. Moses' or 'Madeleine M.' and certainly not 'Mrs. M.' — just 'M'.

'See you Monday, Chicken,' Flo was saying.

'Yeah. See you.' But Ellie's eyes were on the envelope and on the girl's mother, and the girl's mother's eyes were on the envelope, too. Madeleine Moses and Chris Searle hardly looked at each other, and gave each other nothing as treacherous as a smile. Just a businesslike, 'See you at our meeting,' from him, 'Sure!' from her, and Ellie could hardly believe it — he stuck out his hand and shook hers. Which was a big surprise for the lady. And Ellie knew why he'd done that. Oh, yes! She did it herself with some relatives, the whiskery ones, so that there was no extreme possibility of a kiss on the cheek. And, 'See you,' he said again. They were being *too* careful, in front of her.

Flo and her mother went off. While Ellie and her father busied themselves on their different jobs, busy, busy, busy; no room for talk on any level. And it was off up to bed for Ellie, mixed up, more lumpy than ever, puzzling at the scary stuff that Flo had been on about – but absolutely certain now that she was going to have to put her plan into action, first thing on Monday.

CHAPTER SIX

Well before opening time at the Regent's Arms Ellie went through to Commercial Road to get the *Sunday Sport* for her dad. He was one of those men who really did read the lurid press for the sport; he followed football fiercely, and he liked to keep up with who was doing what — mainly his own generation of footballers who had gone into management or coaching; although that sort of career wouldn't have been for him. As a striker he had led his team's attack, but he wasn't a leader off the pitch; he was more of a dreamer; he wasn't loud, and he'd hardly ever in his life pointed an angry finger at anyone. If his blood pressure was going to be a problem one day, it would be for being too low, not too high. So his Sunday morning paper and a cup of coffee at a polished table in the bar – that he dreamed would one day become a smart place to eat – was how he liked to spend the time between checking his kegs and opening the pub at eleven.

Newspapers weren't delivered; Ellie preferred a walk along Commercial Road to get out of the claustrophobia of the Regent's Arms. But today the local newsagent didn't have a *Sunday Sport* so she was forced to go to the small shop along Narrow Street, one in a line of old riverside buildings that backed onto the Thames. And as she hurried home the quicker way, heading for Limehouse Basin, she was suddenly stopped short.

It was the siren sound of Narrow Street moving; a whole section of the roadway swinging aside to let a yacht come in off the Thames and into the lock that connected with the Basin. The swing bridge stopped her physically; but it was something else that stopped her mentally. Right beside her on the pavement was a young Chinese woman with a camera. To all the world she could have been doing the Sunday morning tourist thing and snapping at the high masts of the yacht and the swirl of

the lock water as it ran around the outside of the gates —
typical Limehouse pictures. But she wasn't. What she
was doing made Ellie step back and bring the newspaper
up to cover her face. She was taking long lens shots of
someone Ellie knew.

It was the man who had spoken to her and Flo outside
the Regent on Friday night, the mystery man who had
also been there the week before, looking at the
narrowboats. And now he was sitting on a low wall,
reading his own Sunday paper, as if this was his preferred
Sunday morning thing. Except that every now and again
he was looking over or round the paper — towards the
vessels in the Basin — and being photographed doing so.
What did they call them? Paparazzi? The Chinese
photographer definitely didn't want to be seen by him;
she pretended to shoot in other directions a couple of
times, but she always swung back to the stranger.

Ellie didn't wait for the street to swing back into
place. She turned and ran back the way she had come,
away from the mystery man, before he looked up and saw
her. Who was he? What was his game? Oughtn't her dad
to know about this? But as she clattered back down the
steps and in through the pub door, she asked herself,
what could she tell him? What had she actually got to
report? A bloke she'd seen on the towpath was having his
picture taken?

'Sorry!' she said, out of breath. 'Had to go to another shop.'

'On the other side of the river?' her father asked, his coffee cold.

'I wish!' said Ellie – as she stumped up to her room.

The photographer was in a light jumper and jeans, with bare feet in flip-flops. Her face was shiny and her eyes alert as she took her pictures; until a little nod to herself told her that she had enough, when she slipped her camera away, got onto an old Suzuki scooter, and rode off.

She had a small room above a Cantonese grocery in Ben Jonson Road, where a small table in the window was taken up with a computer. She plugged her digital camera into the USB port and up onto the screen slid all her images of the man by the Basin.

Within minutes, through the satellite bounce of e-mail, Zlatko Matesa sat staring at the same image on a laptop in his room above the Café de Montmartre in Château Renoir-sur-Marne. As he stared at it he lit one of his pungent cigarettes and said something that in any language had to be a swear word. He grabbed at his mobile phone and dialled 0044 followed by a London number, which was answered almost immediately. And in the same tone as the swear word, he told the photographer something very strong — then shut the phone with a loud crack and threw it into a chair.

While her father read his newspaper, Ellie sat at the kitchen table crunching dry cornflakes, too impatient to wait for the milk to soak in. She and her dad had said little to each other all day on Saturday; she'd done a stock check on wines and spirits, crisps, peanuts, and cigarettes in the vending machine; and the rest of the day she'd kept busy, missing badly the old buzz of the home crowd before a Charlton game. She'd done some washing and ironing, heated up a teatime ready-cooked lasagne, with nothing more about her dad's plans being said as they ate it. In the end, someone came into the bar to be served, and Ellie went up to her bedroom to watch rubbish on her television.

But by Sunday morning Ellie finally had something to say, something that she'd been mulling over in those sleepless moments when the mind pans around everything — the vitally important and the trivial.

'Regarding the stock check...' She crunched. She still wasn't getting into a personal chat. 'Tell you what we don't need...'

'No?' He didn't lift his eyes from the page.

'We don't need cigarettes.'

'True,' Chris nodded his head, still into the Premiership, 'we don't shift cigarettes.' Smoking was banned in the pub, but they still had the vending machine for people who couldn't kill the habit and stood outside like leper office workers.

'Well, don't you think that's weird?' Ellie pulled his paper down to engage his eyes. 'You couldn't breathe outside the bar on Friday night, that canal was sizzling with the fag ends thrown in the water... Wonder you never heard it.'

'Yeah, it's got me stuck,' Chris agreed, keeping his place with his finger. 'They must get their fags up the supermarket...'

Ellie helped herself to some more cornflakes. 'I don't reckon they do,' she said. 'We had supermarkets over at Charlton, but we still shifted a few fags ourselves.'

'No? Well, must be day trips to France.' He stayed sociable but his mind was at White Hart Lane.

'Could well be,' Ellie said, 'but not their own trips, I don't reckon. The Friday night crowd's not one big club or anything, they're all themselves, all at their different tables, separate lots wandering up and down outside...' She shook the cornflake packet like percussion for dramatic effect. 'No. I'll tell you what's happening.'

His eyes were wandering back to the paper.

'It's Ivy Stardust. She's bringing cigarettes in.'

Instantly, Chris lost the Premiership – creased it into his lap like a bad result. 'How do you mean?' Now she had him.

Ellie waved her spoon. 'Look, they're all smokers here, Friday nights, right? You could smoke haddock in the air around the Regent – but *we don't sell any fags*! That machine never needs restocking, you haven't had to empty any cash out since we've been here...'

'I won't fault you there...' Chris's interest was one hundred-and-fifty per cent now. He tidied his paper, folded it for later, but his eyes never left hers. 'Go on.'

'Those big speakers in the back corners, they're not connected, they're dead, no sound comes out – and they take two men to carry them in –' Ellie rapped her spoon on the table – 'but it only takes one bloke to carry them away. They're lighter at the end of the night...'

Chris shrugged. 'Where're you going with this?'

Ellie gave him a scornful look. 'I'll tell you where I'm going. That speaker's heavy first-off because *it's stuffed with cigarettes* – coming in. God knows why I'm lying awake working this out, but I'm not in charge of my brain these days.'

'I've never been!'

'Those packs of two hundred, the duty-free size, if you buy in bulk they come in big delivery cartons, a few thousand cigarettes, that'd weigh a bit, take some carrying. And *that's* what I reckon they pay for on the door. Not madam's singing at all.' Ellie hadn't thought this bit out till now, but it could make sense. 'Yeah, they pay Rude Boy on the door for their two hundred, or whatever, he gives them a raffle ticket or two, I've seen it – and no money has to be passed, after that. Then Ivy Stardust sings in short bursts, and in between there's all that moving about, over here, over there, stand up, sit down, while you're kept busy at the bar. The customers take their turns, they wander over to talk to their mates in the corners – but notice it's always the same Watson blokes in the same corners – and it's, 'Give us your raffle ticket,' and then it's hands under the table and under their coats go the fags...'

Ellie's father was sitting up straight with his arms folded like a pre-season photograph. 'Which is why Ivy Stardust doesn't want the plug pulled on her music nights! That councillor reckons her coach firm's dying, and I reckon she keeps it going as a smokescreen for cigarette smuggling...'

'You've got it! Could be, couldn't it?' Ellie hadn't meant to get this excited. 'She's got coaches that go over to France, hasn't she – Disneyland and all that – regular stuff? I've seen it on the side of the Watson coach that drops off outside our school. Kids, families, I bet they get waved through quick as you like at Dover...'

'And fags zipped in the seats, or somewhere...' Chris stretched his neck. 'You're sure about the speaker thing, you've seen it?'

'Well, Flo has, actually... Like, she noticed it first.'

'Clever Flo.' But her father looked away as soon as he said it. 'Clever both of you...'

'Blow all that –' Ellie stood up '– because meanwhile, Christopher James Searle, licensee, you could go down for aiding and abetting a smuggling racket. Prison! Right?'

'Blimey!'

'Yeah, "blimey!", son.'

'But it's only a theory...' Chris's paper was on the floor being trampled.

'Oh, yeah, it's only a theory, like going to prison's a theory till you go in the front door of the Old Bailey and come out through the back to a big white van with black windows! But, fair enough, how it works, it only just came to me in the night.'

Her father was nodding, then showed some compassion. 'Kept you awake, then, sweetheart?'

Ellie eyed him. '*Things* kept me awake. But we can keep a good eye open on Friday, can't we?'

'We can. You bet we can!'

Ellie got up and cleared the table, squirted it with the catering spray, wiped it, and pushed in her chair. It was her kitchen again today. 'And then, when you're sure, you've got to knock it on the head, quick — or tell the police. You've got to be first to the ball, Number Nine, or the law'll put you away with the rest of them...'

Chris Searle narrowed his eyes. 'Has Flo told her mother?'

Ellie shrugged, almost enjoyed her next bitter-sweet words. 'How should I know? Ask her when you see her.' But when Ellie saw the look on his face she went to her dad and gave him a great hug. 'I could be wrong. Perhaps we haven't bitten off a bit more than we can chew, eh?'

Trains were new to Song. Whenever she'd travelled outside Fuchow it was in a 'putong che' bus, cramped and uncomfortable. But this was a 'hard sleeper' train with padded benches and three-tiered bunks for sleeping.

On the long way north to Kaifeng, on buses still, they had stopped at a primitive squatting toilet, where, behind the building, the hard woman from Nanjing had given them their papers – travel permits for a single journey out of China. With that in her hand, and in the daylight, Song's mood brightened. Now that the real journey was under way, the wheels turning, she felt better again, a lot more hopeful than she'd been the night before. She was on her way to a better life, in a country where people could fulfil themselves. She would do what her father had wished for her, right from the time as a little girl when she had stood on the table and sung folk songs to him – to the time near the end when his cancer pained him, but he had still found the strength in his thin hands to clap her. She had been his therapy, she had prolonged his life with her singing for him, and she would bring joy into many hearts when she sang for them in England. 'Special...' was almost the last word that he had said to her.

At Kaifeng railway station they got onto the first of the trains that would take them towards Kazakhstan and Europe – so the woman said, who went ahead along the platform and spoke to someone already on the train, then descended from it, and went away, without any goodbyes. Song had been waiting anxiously; now she needed no goodbye to please her: the note from Uncle Chen must have been okay! And as she and the others climbed aboard the long silver snake, she shivered again, the way she had under the magnolia tree. This long-distance train was going to take her a good way towards her dream.

But once on the train her next shiver was from a nasty, icy blast. His name was 'Boss': he shouted it as he stood over them in the railway carriage, making them sit on the benches. He looked sinister, dark skinned from Mongolia, with a thick helmet of steely hair and a black moustache.

From the start whatever he had to say to them always rode on a curse.

'I tell you "sleep" – you sleep. I tell you "eat" – you eat. I tell you "crap" – you crap. I tell you "no questions ever" – you ask no questions, ever. And this I tell you now! No questions!' His thick black moustache twisted to emphasize his sneer, kept there for each of them as he gave out the tin tags that were their sleeper tickets.

'Men and women together?' the other girl who had travelled from Fuchow asked him, comparing her tag with Lao Zi's, sitting next to her.

Straight off, Boss rounded on her and slapped her face, hard: it sounded like a pistol crack. The girl fell sideways, shocked, a hand to her cheek – but she didn't scream. Everyone stared, but no one moved. Boss would have no need to remind them what his instructions were, nor that he was, indeed, the boss.

With the carriage silent, the train suddenly whistled, and began its journey on the first of what would be many long days. But there were no smiles or 'good lucks' at their pulling away towards their better lives. Conversation had been stifled by Boss's behaviour towards Lin, and also by the presence of a younger woman who was with him, someone they were commanded to call 'Madam Boss' – a white European with a guttural voice and unblinking eyes like a snake's.

After a few hours, meagre food was doled out from a plastic bag, all ten sitting on the benches eating cold boiled rice with their fingers. Song kept her head down most of the time, but her eyes flicked from one to another along the rows, greeted by every face giving out its own mixed message of hope and fear. But no one dared lift a chin or say a word against these two.

Song's eyes went to the windows. Inside the carriage was not a pleasant place to be. But the far mountains made her think of the song of the goatherd that her father had loved – who always pointed a finger at Song's mother when she sang the comic line about the milkmaid who fell off her stool. She saw her mother's face, who also wanted singing success for her, but who kept it inside herself in case those dreams never had a chance to come true. And as the light eventually went from the far mountains and they lost distinction, a rugged beauty outside mingling with the poignant pictures in her head, 'Sleep!' Boss suddenly commanded. Seeming to obey him, the sleeping car's red night lights flickered on, the bunks were pulled down, and, obediently, Song climbed up into her allotted place.

Her hand went immediately to the small charm around her neck, the smooth ceramic peach that her father had brought one day from the market, and hung around her neck as if he were giving her the world on a string: his talisman for good fortune.

Surely, though things were not so good now with Boss and his bullying, this time would pass as time does, and the reward – of England and its opportunities – would be worth it. So, thinking those thoughts against the swaying and rumbling of the train, Song eventually went to sleep – into a new darkness where, for the first time, no dreams came.

Ellie cracked on with her Flo plan first thing on the Monday. Coming to the school from further away than Flo – and eating a smaller breakfast – she usually got there a bit earlier, an edge she could use. So what was more natural than talking to someone in the yard while she was waiting, rather than standing staring at the brick wall? And Jaz Prabhaker was no brick wall to stare at. He had really nice hair, the sort that some girls would die to have, shiny and stylish; a change from the thick convict looks of most boys around there. His eyes were big and brown, and he had the knack of not blinking while he was looking into yours, while his mouth went more naturally to a smile than to a sneer.

As Ellie came into the yard and saw him he was on his own, fishing in his bag for something – so she hurried over and caught him as he stood up. 'I need to say sorry to you,' she said.

'Yeah?' He didn't seem surprised, more half ready for it.

'Last week, I gave you the end of my tongue for something you did...'

'Okay, let's talk ends of tongues...'

Yes, perhaps he was the type Flo said he was. '...I should have said thank you for stopping Watson slapping me.'

'Oh, that.' Jaz went back to fishing for something in his bag. 'Was he?'

Ellie was getting frustrated. This was going all wrong. He was supposed to be being the nice boy she'd met at the cash 'n' carry, seeing her side of things, picking up from where they'd left off, that's the way she'd pictured it in her mind. She shook her head. 'You did know what you were doing, Jaz, and I'm sorry I didn't take it more—'

'Gratefully.'

'Something like that.'

'Whatever.' He looked up at her, and now he did smile as he stood again and faced her, a bagel in his hand. 'Want a bite?' He offered it to her, mouth height. 'They're dead nice.'

Quick decision time. Did she bite Jaz's bagel or did she say she didn't like them? Was she going to stand there and be fed like a little girl, an action saying so much more than it looked, or did she keep her pride? Or just take hold of the bagel in her hand?

'Chicken!' From across the yard Flo was calling, coming over behind Jaz, and wouldn't see who it was for a moment.

Decision made. This was the perfect moment to start carrying out her plan. Ellie bit into the bagel held in Jaz's fingers.

She saw Flo slow down, as she realized who the boy was. She stared at Ellie, who was still chewing, desperately trying to get the dough down while nodding her pleasure at the taste of it.

Jaz looked at Flo and back again at Ellie. 'Would your friend like a bite?' he asked her.

'Dunno,' Ellie managed, a weak voice as she waited for Flo to erupt, to slag her off, to say something hateful to Jaz or to her; because she'd known her plan wasn't going to be any easy little exercise, and she breathed in deeply ready for the assault.

Flo gave no satisfaction, though. Without even a hostile look at Ellie, she turned on her heel and walked away, across the yard to a group of girls by the school steps: while Ellie chewed on the bagel, looking into Jaz's face, and finally finished her mouthful.

Jaz put the rest of the bagel into his own mouth – just as the bell sounded. 'Got some more for break, if you want.' And without waiting for Ellie's response he went, head up high into the building; while Ellie stood for a

115

moment, ashamed to have to wait to start breathing normally before she followed everyone in – because Ellie Searle usually took things as they came, she wasn't the emotional sort, and never mind about Jaz Prabhaker, what she'd deliberately done to a good mate like Flo was well out of order. She was jumping all over Flo's plan to get back with Jaz, plus turning her back on a good friendship of her own – all to stop Mrs. Moses from taking her place with her dad.

Like the saying went, jealousy was a green-eyed monster.

Ellie's parents had always had things out. If there was going to be a row, it blew up sooner rather than later; there weren't a lot of sulks. Other people were different, Ellie knew that. Girls especially. There were never a lot of fights between girls, but war went on all the same. Okay, there were tragic cases in the papers where it was all physical, hard girls and soft targets; but bullying was mostly mental warfare. Girls got shut out of a group, the turned back being more of a weapon than the fist – they weren't picked to be a partner in dance or drama, or for teams at games, not let into a circle in the yard or at the school dinner table; or no one answered when they were spoken to, victims simply weren't there. E-mails were sent, things were whispered behind hands; and if it came to a head the verbals started and they were called a tramp or their mother was called dirty names: which was when the school was asked to take some action, or the kid left, or did something serious to herself... That was what being a girl in school and out of favour could mean.

So how would Ellie feel Flo's bile? How rough a ride was Ellie going to get from Florence Moses? Ellie had thought it through up to here. She'd brought this about, it was part of her plan, her smokescreen, for stopping Flo's mother and her own father from getting too close to each other, but from here she was walking a new neighbourhood. She had never seen Flo in any light other than as a friend; she'd never had to want 'in' with her because that had happened on her first morning – so what Flo would be like as an enemy could only be imagined.

She found out, but it was hard to tell the difference at first. There was no question of sitting in different seats from before; when Ellie went into the form room her place was there, as usual, next to Flo – the girl hadn't gone to sit anywhere else, or invited anyone to sit with her. So, playing her part of the innocent eater of a bite of Jaz Prabhaker's bagel, Ellie sat with her.

When they had to share a book, they shared it: in assembly, the songbooks were one-between-two, and theirs was kept in Flo's desk: she carried it to assembly, and staring to the front, she held it up for Ellie to hold her half. In history they had to make a list of the main World War I battlefields, in order, north to south – and they spoke to each other doing it. In PE they were always a pair, and they were again that Monday, and there was no loose grip or accidental slip. But already by break, Ellie realized that they had said nothing personal to each other, it had all been work. Like that other night when Ellie and her father had cashed up and talked stock, they were the same as any strained couple who had to live with each other and do the same job: friendship was no part of the deal.

Which was just what Ellie wanted, and she hadn't had to say anything unfriendly.

At break time, Flo found her other friends again, but there were no pointing fingers or sniggers – it was as if Ellie just wasn't that important.

Well, not to Flo Moses – because she certainly was to Jaz Prabhaker. He came from the form room and into the canteen area after her, and he already had a bagel in his hand by the time he reached her.

'Yes?' he asked. 'The lady likes? Only I was hoping...'

'You can cut that old rubbish!' Ellie told him. But she smiled and took the bagel to drink with her cone of iced water. She eyed him as she chewed. 'You were hoping what?' She played the eye game harder than ever. 'Hoping *I'll* buy these tomorrow?'

'Nope.' Jaz Prabhaker was nothing if not direct. 'Hoping you'll meet me sometime. What d'you reckon?'

Result! Ellie put on that head-everywhere-round-the-room act to show that she was thinking about it. 'Act' because she *had* thought about it – you don't plan anything without being a move or two ahead, or else it's not planning at all, it's just letting stuff happen. And she wanted to say 'yes' to a question like this. 'Yes' because it would deepen the rift between the Searles and the Moses. And 'yes' because she wouldn't mind, anyway. But something stopped her. Perhaps she'd wait to see how things had gone between her dad and Flo's mother at their meeting. If they were cooling already, perhaps she could get Flo back with a bit of saying sorry. But then it would be Flo as a friend, not a potential stepsister.

'I'll give it a think,' Ellie said.

'Tell us tomorrow? Only I've got stuff I want to say to you.' His voice went down in his throat, came out embarrassed: 'Can't say it in school...'

Something to say to her? That he liked her? That he'd fallen in love with her? Or was what he wanted to say something of the non-verbal sort? Who could know? Anyway, tomorrow was Tuesday when her dad was due to meet Madeleine Moses; she should have some idea by then. 'Tell you Wednesday,' Ellie said.

'Wednesday? You waiting for a better offer?'

CHAPTER SEVEN

The *Watson Travel* Executive Coach pulled up outside the Co-op Hall. It was a dusty old twenty-nine seater, the Watson name painted over something previous, with a registration plate that showed it was ten years old.

It was term-time and the passengers – about eighteen of them – were mostly elderly, the occasional younger man or woman going with a mum or a dad. It was seven a.m. and the middle-aged driver in his crisp white shirt loaded the passengers' smallish suitcases into the luggage compartment. Up in the coach, the guide read out names and ticked them off on his passenger list while people got themselves settled. It was Len Stevens, Ivy's keyboard man, who would occupy the front double seat, doing his occasional day job. His voice was firm, like any old sergeant's, his list was complete – no one was late – and everyone answered up brightly.

'Welcome to your Battlefield Tour,' Len said, as he plonked his folder onto the seat, everyone ticked off. 'Our driver is Mick, he don't like mess, and this is a non-smoking coach, more's the pity. But –' he hunched his shoulders – 'regulations is regulations. We go across the Dartford bridge to the M20 and down to the Channel Tunnel, stop for toilets and a cup of tea' – a small cheer from the back – 'through to Calais on the ol' Shuttle, and south to the Somme, a bite on the way' – another cheer – 'and into Thiepval, where we're staying...'

'Taken, lost, and retaken,' said a pensioner whose grandfather's name was on the memorial there.

Len gave him a nod. 'And I'll keep you up to date all the way, just be sure you're punctual back to the coach when we stop. I hate turning back!'

And in a pleasant mood, the *Watson Travel* two-day tour of World War I battlefields set off, a cheerful party on a sad, memorial trip.

*　*　*

Tuesday was the same for Ellie at school. Jaz Prabhaker brought bagels again, and Flo kept herself to herself. She neither looked at nor commented upon Ellie's cosying up to Jaz, although Ellie did her best to make sure the girl saw what was going on: Flo had been going to give Jaz another chance sometime, so she had to see that he'd moved on. At dinnertime, when Jaz chose a seat in the canteen corner, Ellie moved them to a 'cleaner table' in good view of Flo and her friends. But nothing was made of it, although Jaz looked round a couple of times, as if he guessed that Ellie had ditched her friend for him; but if Flo saw the pair of them together she certainly didn't seem to care. The plan had to be working, though, because again that day, at no time was a personal word said between the two girls, and at the end of it there was no 'see ya', just the scooping up of belongings and a heading off towards home.

Ellie couldn't wait to get back to the Regent's Arms. Her dad and Flo's mother had been having their meeting today and Ellie was dying to know two things: how had it gone in general — and she would know that by the look on her dad's face and the tone in his voice — and had any mention been made of Flo and Ellie, as friends? She was relying on the pair of them not wanting to get all cosy when their kids couldn't stand the sight of each other.

It had been a half past one meeting over 'a bite to eat', with Annie looking after the bar, but when Ellie got in at four o'clock Annie was still the only person in the place. How long did it take two people to have a bite to eat?

'They let you out? No detentions?' Annie asked, polishing a glass to a crystal finish and putting it up above the bar. 'Learn you your ninety-nine times table, did they?'

'Know it already. Is Dad in?' But Ellie knew that he wasn't.

'No, love. Went out an' never come back! An' that was the last we ever see of him — what say we hit the gin?' Already, she was opening a bottle of Coke for Ellie.

'Ta.' Ellie went upstairs and fished out her homework, but her eyes looked nowhere except out of the back window, and her mind couldn't concentrate on anything, not even to pick up a fallen book.

It was past five when her dad came back. He was alone, coming along the towpath from the opposite direction to the Basin, wearing the black suit not seen since Ellie's mother's funeral; but today it was with a matching black shirt and a deep red tie. A deep red face, too, as Ellie went downstairs to face him.

'What time do you call this?' Annie got in before her. 'I've got a dinner to get on, guv'nor.'

'Sorry, Annie,' Chris Searle replied. 'Got into a business discussion.'

Annie straightened. Ellie watched. 'Not about no stupid plans for this place, I hope!' the old barmaid said. She waved her skinny arms around the Regent. 'Works fine, don't it?'

'Sure. No – nothing pacific.' Ellie's dad shook his head vigorously. He'd had a drink, Ellie knew. Wine, probably; he rarely had a real drink, but when he did – and when he had too much – he made mistakes over simple words.

'You all right to take over, then?' Annie asked, doing a final wipe of the bar top.

'Sure. Any trade?'

'A pint for Doggy Dick, an' two joggers who wanted a free glass of water. Told 'em the supply's shut off to stop you putting it in the beer.'

'Cheers.' Chris Searle slid himself out of his jacket, which he threw into the kitchen.

'That's right, hang it on the floor!' Ellie picked up the jacket and put it round a chair. When she went back into the bar her father was wiping a smile off his face. 'So?' she asked.

'So? What?' He looked through her. 'Make us a cup of coffee, Ell, my mind's all befuddled with figures...'

Ellie let go what she might have said – some cheap crack. But while she plugged the kettle in, she asked him:

'Meet up with Mrs. Moses all right, then?'

'I did.'

'And?'

'And I met up with Mrs. Moses.' There was a long pause while Ellie squinted through the crack of the door; he was wiping a wine stain on his shirt with a bar cloth. 'She reckons the plan's a goer, she's going to draw up a list of basic kitchen stuff and fetch the Food Standards documents from Marks and Whatsit. Then she'll come and do a bit of measuring up.'

Ellie's insides had already dropped, from the look of her father there hadn't been any talk from Mrs. Moses about the two girls falling out. Then it was still going forward, the Chris Searle and Madeleine Moses thing, the woman was still 'onboard', as they said: so Flo hadn't been pitching at her to pull out. 'Where'd you go? For your bite to eat?'

'Italian place, Narrow Street.'

'Oh – a rival place? Sussing it out?'

'There's room for two. Anyhow, it's more hard edges and shiny lights than I want. I want cosy, intimate, your friendly canal-side venule.'

'Venue,' she corrected.

'That's right.'

'With an Italian menule, I suppose?'

'You got it.' He took off his tie and hung it like a long

tongue over a lamp bracket. 'But we'll keep our eyes skeeled Friday,' he added, staring at Ellie as she brought him his cup of coffee. 'Decide how to play it.' He nodded to himself.

'I'm glad it went okay,' Ellie lied. 'Long time, though, weren't you?'

'Oh,' her father waved his hand in the air dismissively, 'we had a coffee at her place...' But he couldn't keep a little smirk off his face.

'Did you now?' That was in the completely opposite direction to where they'd eaten. But she didn't want to hear any more about it. Him back at her place! On their own! Up to now there had always been people about, now it was coffee for two, background music, and a soft settee, no doubt!

Ellie suddenly left him to it and stumped off upstairs, not to do her homework – she couldn't concentrate on that even more than she couldn't concentrate before – but to lie on her bed and make an important decision: that she definitely had to ratchet up the Flo break-off; she'd got to 'up' the stakes, bring things to a nasty head.

So she *would* go out with Jaz Prabhaker, and show Flo how you couldn't afford to be too confident that a good-looking boy was going to wait for you to come round. See if that couldn't do the trick. Get her wanting to be three rows of desks away – and her mother three hundred miles.

In Limehouse Basin the *Laughing Lady* was untying ready to leave on the morning tide. She was a white and blue cabin cruiser, twelve metres long, with a smart and shiny bridge, a decent-sized main cabin, bedrooms fore and aft, a dinette galley, and a deep draught. It was more comfortable than luxury, and its owner and skipper, Hector McLeish, was supervising his deckhand while his wife Myra sipped at a Buck's Fizz in the wheelhouse. The McLeishes were just the sort of boating people that Chris Searle would like to attract to his new canal-side restaurant when it opened, and Madeleine Moses had reckoned that it would be a good idea to talk to some of these people quite soon – build up a bit of interest.

'Find your market, do your homework, see where the beans is, an' maybe get some backers. Float yourself, like they say, the same as on the stock market.' And then she'd whooped with laughter at the word 'float' and drawn plenty of attention to herself in the restaurant.

Chris Searle wouldn't get at the *Laughing Lady* people today, though. As the sun rose, casting the long shadow of Canary Wharf over Limehouse, before too many sharp eyes were about, they were taking their cruiser through the Basin lock and out into the high-tide Thames, heading across into the right-hand shipping lane and off down the

River Thames towards the sea. You had to be up early to catch the *Laughing Lady*.

Ellie told Jaz Prabhaker the good news he'd been waiting for. That same Wednesday morning she found him in the yard again – she knew where he'd be – and his eyes were full of question.

'Yeah,' she said.

'You mean it? You'll see me an' let me talk to you?'

'I said "yeah", didn't I?' Ellie told him. 'Depends where, and what time, and all that, though.'

Jaz had thought it out. 'Mile End Park,' he said. 'You walk up the canal from your place. There's a lock there, I'll meet you by the lock. Tomorrow, Thursday, 'bout half six.'

Ellie pretended to think about it, but in her head she knew exactly what she was going to say. 'Not sure about tomorrow. Could be cash 'n' carry. I could do tonight...' Because it was the sooner the better now for Ellie. She wanted time for Flo's mother to be put off going to the Regent's Arms on Friday by Flo, and Friday itself would be too late.

Jaz narrowed his eyes at her. But if he thought she was being eager he didn't crow about it. 'Okay, I can do tonight, I'll sacrifice India v. Australia cricket.'

'Big of you.' Ellie glanced as casually as she could around the yard, looking for Flo — she wanted her connections with Jaz to be well seen; and she knew that Mile End Park up the canal wasn't far from Flo's place; she'd make sure she was seen there tonight by other kids from the school. But this morning Flo had to be inside already or not come yet, because the only significant person Ellie saw was Rude Boy Watson, who was leaning against the wall of the boys' outside lavatories, picking at a zit. And eyeballing her and Jaz Prabhaker.

'Want a bagel?'

Ellie came back to Jaz. 'Could I say something about bagels?' she asked him.

'You don't like bagels?'

'Don't want to look like one.'

'What about chapattis?'

Ellie laughed. 'You want me as fat as Flo?' she asked.

At which Jaz laughed, but said nothing.

Song's feet were bleeding. Her shoes weren't as strong as she'd thought, and the soles were thin. Uncle Chen had said nothing about boots: he'd talked about travelling by train and bus and truck and boat, but he'd said nothing of what Song was having to do now.

After a week going westwards, train after train, halt

after halt, they'd come near to the Kazakhstan border, where Boss suddenly told them that there might be trouble with their papers – so they were going to have to climb through a mountain pass. He must have known this all along: but when their faces showed surprise, he pushed them off the train at a halt, and led the way, fast, into nearby trees. They had to run to keep up, but that was not the worst of it. The hard climb that started soon after was along a mountain track where jagged rocks and sliding shale made Song's muscles ache and her feet start to bleed in her cheap shoes. Boss and the woman both had boots and mountain walking sticks, which they used for the steep track and for prodding the slow movers, but the rest were unprepared for the arduous trek.

Lin, who walked and climbed behind Song in the line, seemed even worse off than the others. She was older than Song but a smaller girl, frail, and very vulnerable – her eyes would dart at the sight of the smallest bird – and Song wondered why someone like her had chosen to come on such a journey. But she didn't ask. Whenever the young people started to talk, Boss shut them up, tried to keep them isolated in their own skins, so she knew nothing of Lin's story. But Song saw a look that came into Lin's eyes from time to time, a sort of distant yearning for something that wasn't just of England ahead. It was the way Song's mother sometimes stared out across the fields when she thought she was unseen, towards the cemetery and the reunion that would come one day. So almost from nostalgia, ever since that first hard slap from Boss, Song had tried to keep an eye on Lin, lent her a pulling hand, said cheerful things when the going was steepest.

With stick and boots, Madam Boss led at a fast pace. Boss himself was at the rear to bully and prod as the short line of climbers slipped, twisted and fell on the narrow upward track, where eagles wheeled high above – but mostly unseen as Song's neck ached with the constant staring at the ground for the next safe foothold. Rocks reached out and grazed her, stones gave way underfoot, someone up front could start a small avalanche back down the track to cut her shins and legs. It was one gruelling step at a time – and for Song to stop to bind a bleeding wound was to be called a stupid, ungrateful drain rat, and to 'Get on! March!' – with a cuff and another prod from the stick.

The only married pair in the group helped each other, well in the middle of the line; everyone else was for themselves, except for Song sometimes helping Lin, who wept as she climbed; and when they came to a flatter stretch before a descent, she begged Boss to let her stop, to go no further. 'Leave me here! Leave me here!' But he shouted and swore at her, and would have hit her if Song hadn't pulled her out of reach.

All day they followed the ups and downs of the mountain pass – and only when the sun disappeared and they couldn't see their way in the dark any more did Boss allow them to stop for the night. Song sat and nursed her sore feet, ripped the tail off a shirt in her rucksack to wrap around them. But there was no comforting Lin. She whimpered and whimpered about wanting to be left, until Song quietened her with a soft lullaby – before Madam Boss could come cursing to her. They ate their rations of rice, and slept huddled through a shivering mountain night, to be awoken at dawn and prodded on.

It was freezing cold. None of Song's shivering was with a joyful thrill any more: no – Uncle Chen had not prepared her for these conditions. She hadn't thought it would be easy, travelling overland to Europe, but the names painted red in the village hall had made her think only of the final arrival – although, in truth, she knew none of those names well enough to have heard tell of their new lives. She had only imagined that they'd all found happiness and fulfilment. Now she was finding out that attaining such a goal meant deprivation, discomfort – and debasement.

They spent three days like this, through endless mountain, nothing improving, until the blessed memory of a hard train seat seemed as distant to Song as her childhood. And when the long descent began it was so steep in places that the forward pressure on her toes hurt her feet more than the climb. But now at least there was a target in sight – the far-off river that marked the border. Down and down they slid and clattered, her backside taking the injuries now, with cries and curses from them all that covered poor Lin's distress, who was wailing now on every breath.

Suddenly, everyone stopped. No warning. The sound of shots froze them. A volley rang out, ricocheting and echoing, and very, very near. Boss ran to the front and took over the lead, moving them on fast again around an outcrop of the mountain. Madam Boss dropped to the back, swiping with her stick whenever the pace was too slow, and curses flew from one to another along the line to keep up speed or the last one suffered. Which, despite Song's efforts, was mostly Lin. More volleys sounded as they were whipped and kicked along; until, after a painful half-hour, Song realized that the shooting had stopped; all that could be heard was the sound of their own movement. And it came to her how sinister the sound of silence could be, the absence of the echoing shots was scary. Were the soldiers or guards or bandits getting closer, or moving further away?

Suddenly, she knew. Where the track led round a steep descending bend, Boss stopped abruptly at its point. Forcefully, he signalled the line to halt and to keep their mouths shut. From his belt he took his field glasses which he focused on the line of trees that lay below them. Song could see where he was looking: and there, heading into the firs, was a line of soldiers in khaki, about ten of them, with rifles slung from their shoulders. Boss waved the party to crouch and stay still and silent. From that position, Song couldn't see into the trees any more; she just had to stay still while today's fresh blood began to seep through her bandaged split soles and onto the stony path.

When she thought she couldn't stay like that another second, at last the order came. 'We go!' They could move again. Faster now, almost at a run, Boss led them down the final twists of the mountain path and across a stretch of scrubland into the fir trees. He seemed to be certain that the soldiers had gone from the wood because he paid no heed to the noise the travellers made any more. Startled birds could fly up, hidden creatures could scuttle, twigs could crack and snap. With whipped branches in her face and debris in her shoes, Song hurried through the wood with the others, to the left, to the right, straight ahead, ducking, falling, on and on down through the screening of leaves that was becoming lighter and lighter. To be suddenly halted by Boss again as they came to open country.

'Border!' he barked, pointing ahead with his stick – at the river that Song had seen from the mountain, which looked no different from any other river, no wires, no fences, no marking buoys, as far as the eye could see, unguarded along its bank.

So they had reached their first border – this river that ran a hundred metres wide between them and the first foreign country that they must cross, Kazakhstan, but only after they had crossed the river itself...

This close it looked terrifying. From the mountain it had been a feature of the landscape, like a picture seen in a school book. Now, down here, with its vastness before her, with the rush and turmoil of the water, the speed of the tree stumps and swirls of grass and roots skiffing past, the deafening, unremitting sound of the flow, the river was like an angry grey beast.

'Not deep!' Boss growled. 'Is why we cross here.'

But Lin had gone rigid. 'Let me stay! Go back! I beg!' she screamed.

Boss just hit her, another smack across the face.

'I can't swim, I'm scared of water!' she cried – and he hit her again.

Song couldn't stop him, just felt the welling up inside of a scalding rage.

'You don't swim, stupid pig! You put your rucksack on here –' he hit his head with a great thwack – 'and you walk. Boss knows the causeway.'

There must have been recent rains, though, because

the water was high and the current was strong. As they went to the riverbank the flow swirled forcefully at their feet, and it struck so cold that Boss had to herd them in like a rustler. 'Go! In! Follow Madam.' He made free with his stick. 'Go! Walk direct behind!' And, ruthlessly, he pushed the terrified Lin in first. She fell, went under, panicked, and would have gone with the current if Song hadn't grabbed her, fast. She pulled Lin to her feet, choking and spluttering and screaming and hitting out at Song. But Song held her firmly and shouted that everything would be all right – she would get them both safely across.

By now the line had gone on, one after the other, the river up to their chests or their necks, a hand for the current and a hand for their rucksacks. Song took the terrified girl forward, the eye-level river looking almost a world wide. Madam Boss was leading the way, Boss swimming and circling them with fierce eyes and teeth like a crocodile.

Song walked on the slip and slime of the river bed. Somehow, she had a hand for the rucksack on her head and a hand for Lin – and when the river deepened in the middle and she was up on her toes, she just about managed to support the girl enough to keep both their heads above the water. But when the current really wanted to pull them downriver, and their cheeks were

*pressed tight against each other, Lin found breath to cry
into Song's face, 'I want to die!'*

*'No!' soothed Song. 'We're more than halfway across,
we're getting there – and you're not going to drown!' She
pulled Lin on, away from those thoughts.*

'I'm not fit for this,' Lin whimpered. 'Let me die!'

*Song took the moment to kiss the girl on the forehead.
'It will all be all right,' she said. 'You won't want to die
in England.' But as she guided Lin to the other shore, she
might have added, 'If we ever get there...'*

The weather was good and the *Laughing Lady* was
making good time. She had hugged the Kent shore and
emerged into the estuary, passing Sheerness on her
starboard side and heading on to give a wide berth to the
Walpole Rocks off Cliftonville, arced round Foreness
Point, to head south for the run down to Dover.

From here it had been the open sea and the two busiest
shipping lanes in the world, the English Channel through
the narrow Straits of Dover. By now it was getting late-
afternoon dark and Ken, the *Laughing Lady's* young
Chinese deckhand and general dogsbody had his eyes raw
on lookout duty. In the gathering dark and with a sea
mist curling up, an oil tanker the size of an aircraft
carrier could run down a cabin cruiser without seeing her

— and it was the small vessel's safety obligation to keep the sharper lookout. Which wasn't just the boy. People like the McLeishes who regularly crossed the Channel had up-to-the-minute radar and satellite tracking devices onboard.

The only thing they didn't do was make a big show of themselves. Radio silence was a favourite state aboard the *Laughing Lady*. Soon, though, they would be across the shipping lanes and close to the coast of France, where they did most of their business.

The walk up to Mile End Park was short, but Ellie still couldn't make it quickly enough. She felt safe from a mugging point of view, she would never use her mobile phone in a lonely place — she kept it on a chain round her neck, tucked inside her top — and she didn't carry a purse or a shoulder bag, everything was in the pockets of her leather jacket, except for a small plastic bag with two doughnuts that she'd bought on the way home from school: well, Jaz liked stodge, didn't he? And she hadn't dressed up tonight: just a touch of make-up as if she was meeting a mate from school — which is what she'd told her dad — so there was no way she looked glam like Flo on a Friday night. There were places in the area where it wasn't safe for girls to walk alone, and she wasn't sure about further up the towpath so she took no chances.

But it wasn't people Ellie was worried about. It was the constant presence of the canal that bugged her. Now, as usual, she walked on the inside edge of the towpath, always letting people pass her on the outside, because the thought of an accidental slip into that water had become an obsession with her. She used to swim – she'd been a fair swimmer without being a star – but she had a terrible picture in her head, she'd had it ever since they'd moved here, and that was of her mother floating past face up like Ophelia. Now anything that disturbed the surface of the Regent's Canal was a potential victim of drowning until Ellie had seen what it really was. Which was a stupid state to be in, she knew. A look at a globe showed that the world was mostly water, and Ellie Searle had to live in this world, not in some dry paradise garden – so the sooner she got over this terrible phobia, the better.

Meanwhile the sooner she got to Mile End lock the better, too.

She wanted to get there and get herself seen by any Limehouse High kids out in the park while it was light. And as for Jaz Prabhaker? Well, she didn't want to be late on a first date...

But he wasn't there at the lock when she arrived. And there was no one else over the road in the park when she looked – well, no one who would count in Ellie's plan; just a dog being thrown a ball by a heavyweight who looked like a wrestler. There were no kids to see her, and the light was beginning to go, so they all had to be indoors watching television. Ellie checked her watch. No, she wasn't early; Jaz Prabhaker was late, or he was a 'no show', which he'd better not be!

She went back to the lock, looked up and down the towpath, but she didn't know where Jaz lived, so she wasn't sure which direction to look in, even.

And then she heard him call her; 'Ellie', in a muffled sort of voice, and when she looked back up to the road bridge that crossed the canal, Jaz Prabhaker was there, where she hadn't expected him to come from, waving an arm and hurrying down to her.

Well, better late than never! At least she hadn't been stood up.

But even as he came puffing along the towpath towards her, she could see that there was something wrong. His face was puffy, one eye seemed smaller than the other, and his mouth was fixed in a twisted attempt at a smile.

'Jaz!'

'Ellie.' His wince told her he couldn't say it without it hurting. He spat blood onto the ground.

'Jaz! What's happened to you?'

And the pathetic thing was, he was still trying to smile. 'Wayne Watson happened to me. That's...what.'

'Wayne Watson?'

'He jumped me, him and two others...'

'Jaz! That's terrible! For protecting me – that's what that is! That's my fault!' Ellie wanted to touch Jaz's swollen face, to do something to make him feel better. 'You are going to the police?'

'Hell I am! This was nothing. This was what he called the friendly warning...'

'Warning? Warning about what?'

'No, not warning *about*, warning *to*...'

'*To?*'

'To anyone who upsets him. He reckons.'

Ellie looked all around her, as if by staring north, south, east and west she might get her head round all this business. A warning to him? A warning to her? Had Watson beaten up Jaz because he'd stopped that swipe the other day?

'Jaz, you've got to tell the police! This is serious, this isn't school and playground, and kids' fights...'

Now Jaz gripped Ellie's arm. 'I don't say nothing, you don't say nothing.' He had to wince on everything he said. 'This is done. But this is nothing...nothing to what *could* be done.' His twisted, beaten face came closer, not handsome tonight but grotesque. 'Ell, his sort of people break arms, legs, stab, shoot, *kill*! Ask my people, they know. No, whatever this is about, nobody says nothing, you got me? Police are useless!' And he spat blood onto the towpath again.

Ellie didn't know what to say or what to think. 'Well, thanks for coming out looking like that! You didn't have to.' Which she hadn't meant to seem cruel and light-hearted, but Jaz's larger eye seemed to twinkle. 'What I mean is, I'm grateful.'

Jaz shook his head, winced again. 'You'd have been hanging about, and I've got no money on my mobile...I want you to know I'm all right...like, as a person.'

'Of course you are.'

'And I really wanted to see you. I wanted to talk to you.' He sat on the wide sluice arm at the lower end of the lock.

'Yeah, that's nice, I wanted to see you, too. But the way things are...'

'The way things are? You're here, I'm here. So we can talk. I want to say some things.' He was looking at the stone slabbing at his feet.

'Okay. Shove up.' Ellie went to sit next to Jaz on the sluice arm, but she wanted to stay on the land side, not the water. What was this, though? When people went out together they walked, they had a laugh: they talked, yes – but talking wasn't the big deal; it was the just being with the other one. But all Jaz was ever on about was seeing her to talk to her. Anyway, she sat, quite close to him.

He was still staring at his feet. 'What I wanted to ask you to do...'

He looked up, looked round the neighbourhood the way Ellie had earlier, bringing himself to his point.

Ellie stiffened. *What he wanted her to do?* So Flo had been right, he *was* a brash piece of work. Being all formal, asking permission to do something! What was in his leery head? She suddenly felt a weird churn in her stomach about what he was going to say.

'Flo.'

'What about her?' Ellie was sitting up very straight.

'I was stupid with her, it wasn't just me, I thought she wanted—'

'What? What are you trying to say?' Ellie had stood up now. She hadn't come here to talk about Flo.

Jaz didn't move. 'I just wondered if you could...tell her I'm not a villain, that's all. Tell her you an' me get on okay, and I'm all right. I've not tried anything on, have I, an' I wouldn't any more.' His face looked pained, saying the words, and a further thought shone in his good eye. 'I've taken a beating for you, and you can do me a favour in return...'

'Yeah?'

'I want you to ask her if she'd go out with me again.'

Ellie stared at him. She wouldn't have blinked if a mosquito had flown into her eye. She knew her mouth was open but she couldn't shut it. The dog! The crud! The muck off the bottom of her shoe! What cheek was this? Chatting her up, stopping Rude Boy Watson from swiping her, feeding her up with his stupid bagels, asking her out as if they were on a date – and all to get round her to get round Flo!

Right now she felt like adding to his injuries! Except for one thing – which she could recognize despite her anger. They'd both been using each other for their own little plans, hadn't they?

Words failed her, plus any thought of what to do. So in frustration she opened the bag of doughnuts, threw one into the bushes and one at his stupid head. 'Have that!' she said – and she stomped off down the towpath; angry, humiliated, and even, yes, disappointed that Jaz hadn't wanted to try anything on with her that he'd tried on with Flo.

So now she had neither of them; neither Jaz nor Flo; just her dad – no mum – and the rotten Regent's Arms, which was at the rock bottom of all their troubles here in Limehouse.

It was ten o'clock that evening when the minibus arrived on the outskirts of Château Renoir-sur-Marne. Zlatko

Matesa was at the wheel, with ten young people behind him, all sleeping like anyone would who'd just done a double shift at Disneyland. They were all leaning into each other, bumping their heads on windows, but not rousing.

When they got to the rooming house in the Rue de Noyer, Matesa stopped with a brutal foot on the brake, sending them all forward into those in front. With gestures and a few international swear words he offloaded his passengers and unlocked the front door for them. And within a quarter of an hour he was at his table in the Café de Montmartre, eating a plate of *frites,* drinking his poisonous-looking glass of something green, and smoking, smoking, smoking throughout.

Eventually he went, calling in at a nearby *créperie* for a box of plain *crépes* and a bottle of cider, and made his way back to the rooming house where he let himself in with a short, sharp shout of *'Ishrana!'* – as if he were a hard boss doing no more than throwing food at his band of workers.

all; but at least the walking was over, and Song's feet would have some relief. There were air vents in the canvas sides, and flatter sacks of cotton to lie on, basic comforts after those arduous mountain days. But Song's greatest relief was to see the back of Boss and his woman.

When they had burrowed through the back of the lorry, the driver replaced the disturbed bales of cotton and shut them in, warning them in English, 'Remember, you got in here yourselves. I am clean. You make noise, the lorry is searched, you go to prison, not Riz. And prisons here –' he had shown three gold teeth as he grinned – 'they are not so good.'

Even as Song was still finding her own cramped space, the frame of the lorry shook with the start of the engine, and the next part of her journey began with her still kneeling, like an animal going to market. Lin, whose whimpering had lessened as her clothes had dried on her, moved herself to sit next to Song, their legs outstretched.

Soon, Lin slept; but Song couldn't sleep. Swaying and bumping under the dim, swinging light, she saw in her head what she had seen so many times since her father had died: she saw herself singing for him, but not alone, for others, too: for her mother beside him, and for an audience of friends and familiar faces that listened to the words, and took comfort from them. A teacher of singing

who had once come to Fuchow had said, 'The words of a
song can dress the wounds of the audience.' Her singing
could do that, Song knew, and was all part of what she
wanted to give. Yes, some songs are sad songs, and these
help to mend a broken spirit; but others are joyful, and
reach to high octaves of hope. And this was the song in
her heart that night: a new song of future dreams: which,
if she had to give it a name, would be entitled 'England'.

School was a worse place to go that Thursday morning
than Ellie had ever thought it could be. She had to drag
her feet along Salmon Lane, down White Horse Road,
and force herself to go in through the gates of Limehouse
High. There was no one in here whom she'd be pleased to
see. She longed, as she'd never longed, for her old
Charlton school, her eyes almost misting with tears at the
thought of the friendly south London faces she wouldn't
see today. They were all in the past: she'd exchanged a
couple of text messages with lifelong mates, but the latest
of hers had brought no reply. Life moves on. She didn't
expect Jaz Prabhaker today, he'd be nursing his swollen
face, but Rude Boy Watson would be here smirking the
most innocent of looks – until he came over and repeated
his threats. So what would she do then? Talk big about
going to the police? Would she dare?

And Flo? Ellie still didn't know what she thought about Flo. Flo had done her no wrong, it was Ellie who was trying to force a break-up, and unbelievably the girl hadn't stooped to being nasty back: just distant. And what of Jaz Prabhaker's message for Flo? Would she deliver it? Would she doughnuts!

So why didn't she just take Flo on one side and tell her everything? Tell her why she'd made a play for Jaz; let her know how she'd feel about her dad and Flo's mum being an item so soon, how she wasn't ready for that yet – because her own mother hadn't been dead a year. But would Flo listen? Would she understand? Could Ellie take that risk? And how would she feel if Flo *did* give Jaz another chance: where would she be then, even down to where she sat in the form room?

Questions, questions. And in the way people do when there's a lot hanging on things, Ellie decided to do nothing. She'd just get through another day at Limehouse High and see what happened. Who knew, she might accidentally fall out of a third-floor window and that would be that, wouldn't it?

All this gave one reason for the churning going on inside her. But there was another reason – the one that got her heart thumping fast when she thought about it, made her catch her breath whenever she remembered what she was carrying in her school bag – and that was the start of a new session of lessons that began today. Costume and towel for six weeks' intensive course.

Swimming. At St George's Pool.

It was really for non-swimmers, a sort of remedial course for newish arrivals to Tower Hamlets, because most of the rest had learned to swim at primary school. But for a borough on the river, and with a canal running through it, the Education Authority laid on these intensive courses for non-swimmers — and Ellie had deliberately lied. She guessed that being a swimmer or not wasn't one of those educational records that followed you from school to school; at any rate, it wasn't the sort of thing that would jump out at a tutor. So when she'd been asked the question a couple of weeks before, when she'd been well in with Flo and feeling better about herself than she did now, she'd gone for it. It was a chance to start her fight against her fear of water, to be in safe hands with nothing expected of her in the shallow end of a swimming pool. A gutsy decision: but now she was committed to it. And she dreaded it.

In a way, though, it solved her problem of how she'd feel sitting next to Flo all morning — because Flo could swim, she knew. She swam for her house, would probably swim for the school. 'Chicken! Can't you swim?' she'd asked when Ellie had put her name down for the lessons. 'It builds your muscles; builds everything!' And she'd stuck out her chest and screeched with the laugh that Ellie was now missing so badly. Today, though, shortly after registration, Ellie was called out of the form room and went to the yard to line up for the coach. With neither a word nor a look from Flo as she went: she was cool, that girl.

And the coach, when it pulled up? *Watson Travel!* Of course, it had to be! Some things in life you never escaped.

The swimming pool was divided into two by a floated rope. The Limehouse High non-swimmers were in the shallow end, and a group of men working in pairs was in the deep end, rescuing one another, doing resuscitation on the side – taking some sort of certificate in life saving. All very safe – but as Ellie walked out of the changing room and looked down at the pool, just for a second she thought she would faint. Since her mother had drowned she had only showered, not taken a bath, and she had not seen clear water in any sort of capacity for months. Today as she looked down at the empty end of the pool, lining up for the instructor to check names and lay down the rules, all she could see under that clear, wriggling surface was that image she had of her mother – lying peaceful, eyes closed, about to come up any second and say, 'Ellie!' – but be dead all the time.

'Searle? Are you deaf, girl?' The swimming teacher

had to be a female instructor of the old school or she might have considered the possibility that Ellie *was* deaf.

'Sorry.'

'So you're here? Good. Pay attention, girl. *I* can swim. *You* can't.'

Some people just asked to be pushed in, and this small, pinched, white woman with scarlet lips and mascaraed eyes – waterproof no doubt – was crying out for it. But Ellie was here for her own purposes, although right now she could easily have turned tail and run off out of this place. She stared at the woman, and nodded.

'Right!'

And, jerked out of her reverie, Ellie's lesson began. Of course she walked down the steps instead of jumping in, and she took a long, nervous time doing that. The chill of the water was nothing, but what made her start breathing shallow and fast was the gradual rise of it up her legs and around her waist as she went down the steps, to stand with her head and shoulders well out of the water. So far she was not alone; the others were all novices. But now they were instructed to put their shoulders under and cling first to the bar for some leg kicking, and then hold on to a polystyrene float. Gradually, shutting her eyes, steeling herself, Ellie managed to do as she was told – as she was wanting to do – but the sweat breaking out on a cold body in cold water had her shivering at the stress of this moment. But she conquered it. Ellie had always had guts, she hadn't *had* to come here to do this, and she found herself some mental images to give her strength. She was an evacuee doing this lesson at a hostile country school; she was a refugee from a terrible war, swimming across a river to freedom; she was a French Resistance worker, paddling to plant a bomb beneath the hull of an enemy battleship. She was anything and everything where any courage was called for, and she met her own standard. She submerged to her shoulders and with eyes more shut than open, her teeth gritted so hard she'd feel it in her jaws all day, she did what she was told. She held her mouth sealed tight to the water; when she opened her eyes she didn't look down, but up at the high glass roof; and when she braved herself to extend her arms and use the float she was congratulated for a good style of kick, had no trouble getting from one side of the pool to the other. Being in the water up to her shoulders she could manage, somehow it wasn't the same as imagining herself floating backwards under its surface, face up. She hated it, but she coped.

Until the final part of the lesson. The swimming teacher was crouching at the poolside with her fifteen water novices holding the bar, all standing up and facing her.

'Shoulders under!' she commanded — and they all

crouched down again, Ellie almost as quickly as the rest. 'The hardest part for a new swimmer is getting their face under,' the woman told them. 'You've all had them stuck out like dogs in a pond.' A little titter along the bar. 'But you can't feel at home in the water with your head sticking up. All beginners want it, but you can't keep your face dry, swimming. Swimming properly, you're under as much as you're out, you're creatures of the water, the water is your medium – so we're going to get used to being under it...'

At those words Ellie could feel herself going light in the head again, so hard was her grip on the bar that her hands were hurting. *Being under it.* And she knew that this was what she'd come for.

'So you're going to take a deep breath, and put your face in the water, not even up to your ears, and you're going to bubble for me. Bubble.' And the teacher made a bubbling sound, putting on the look to go with it that got the class laughing again. Except Ellie.

'All right – a big breath, and down we go! Under! And bubble!'

The line of non-swimmers went down: some quickly, some slowly, some quite eagerly, some reluctantly, some not bothered by it, some facing down their fears. Bubble, bubble, bubble – it sounded like a line of Cola drinkers misbehaving with their straws. But Ellie wasn't among them. She looked at the water, stared into it, she closed her eyes, she opened them, and still all she could see under there was the serene face of her mother, disfigured by the agitated surface.

And she couldn't do it. Evacuee, refugee, Resistance worker, she couldn't make it work. This was the moment she'd come for, and no way could she bring herself to do it. This was the crunch, and want to do it as she did, will it as she might, she couldn't bring herself to put her face into that water.

'Come on, girl — don't be scared, it won't bite!'

On the side, all Ellie could see were the scarlet-nailed toes of the swimming teacher as her own body shivered in the cold water.

Do it! Do it! She closed her eyes and prayed. *Please God help me to do it!* Because she had to do it for herself — and for her mother. Her mother wouldn't want her to be petrified like this; her mother wouldn't want to be the cause of some serious phobia over water.

But Ellie couldn't. Just couldn't. She surrendered and stood up out of the water, openly crying now, and trembling, and shaking her head.

'All right.' And suddenly there was a whisper of compassion from the woman. 'Next week, eh? Have a go in your sink, or in your bath —'

Which was when Ellie broke down completely: she

could never face a full bath of water. She fell forwards onto the poolside and had to be pulled up out of the pool by the teacher. To be suddenly shocked by a whoop coming from the other end of the pool.

'Men! Adults!' the swimming teacher scorned. 'You beginners are perfectly behaved, and grown men are prancing about like silly schoolgirls!'

There was another whoop as a couple more of the adult class came from the locker room wearing their pyjamas, the clothes they'd have to take off treading water as part of their Bronze Medallion in life saving.

'Where's your teddy, Alan?' one of them shouted.

And Ellie stared: rubbed her eyes and stared: because one of the men in the pyjamas had a face she knew; one of them was the stranger she and Flo had seen and spoken to out on the towpath by the Regent's Arms, who knew that she was the owner's daughter. The man who'd been secretly photographed at the Basin. Ellie looked hard at the teacher.

'Police!' the woman said. 'Acting like kids!' Ellie leaned forward again to stare at the men. 'That's what they do with ratepayers' money! Lark about!'

And Ellie sank down the wall to sit hunched and bewildered on the side as the teacher gave the others permission for five minutes' free time.

Police! That man was police! So what was a

policeman doing hanging about outside the pub two Fridays in a row? Was she right about the dodgy cigarettes – and the police were on to it? And was her dad in line to be pulled in with the under-the-counter gang?

She shivered.

'Get a towel, girl!' the swimming teacher ordered. 'Or go and get changed!'

But Ellie stayed huddled. It wasn't the chill that had given her the shivers.

People have various reasons for visiting the World War I battlefields; some educational, some personal, some to hang a reason on a couple of days away. In the *Watson Travel* party, Jack had a great-uncle buried in a mass grave somewhere near the lines of white headstones in Pargny British Cemetery on the Somme. And that Thursday evening Jack was there a kilometre south of the village of Pargny, holding something wrapped in a cloth in his hand.

'Okay,' said Len Stevens, 'so this is your Pargny British Cemetery. Over six hundred men whose resistance held up the German advance across the Somme – three-quarters of them unidentified...'

'Not Jack's uncle, though.'

'No, not Jack's uncle – an' we're goin' to find his gravestone...'

'Fusilier Albert Lewis,' Jack put in.

And as the dusk had fallen, the party had walked the lines of headstones, and with the help of a chart showing the numbered plots and the alphabetical rows, Jack and his wife had found the sad memorial to Great-Uncle Albert.

Len Stevens left the party to their own thoughts as they stared silently at the old-fashioned names that might live on for ever in this small corner of the Somme.

Len made his own way to the imposing memorial cross at the far end of the cemetery, and as he walked towards it an eerie sound rose up from the cemetery. It held him; it held everyone. It was Jack Lewis blowing the bugle that he had taken from its cloth, that he had tucked into his overnight bag for this purpose. He was sounding the Last Post, the traditional salute to the dead soldier. Nobody moved; the surprise, and the emotion of the moment, stilled them all as they thought of past family members who might have marched through this countryside, to the slaughter, and of their grandsons now who would be the right age to be cannon fodder.

But Len seemed to be waiting for something else; and with everyone's attention on the Last Post, he took the chance to slip out of sight of the party, behind the memorial. Now his head twisted to the sound of a low, urgent whistle from the trees beyond. Immediately, a figure came out of the foliage and across the smooth cut grass, walking with an angry purpose. His eyes, as he came nearer, stared at Len with menace, and his stained teeth, clenched around a foul-smelling, yellow cigarette, were bared like a feral cat's.

'You got a problem!'

'No problem. Everything's okay our end. Envelope's in me pocket.'

'You tell your people –' But some men can't whisper, and he was shushed by a wet-eyed woman who was closer to the memorial than Len had thought. '– this business does not stop! Okay?' Zlatko Matesa was not a man to be shushed.

Len Stevens took his arm and led him a few metres away. The last notes from Jack's bugle wound down to its grieving end. There was a silence while people weren't sure whether or not to clap – so they coughed and shuffled their feet instead.

'No problem. I told you, everything's okay and I've got your money for the last lot.' If Len Stevens had his doubts about the new set-up at the Regent's Arms, his eyes didn't show them. 'Why should we put the tin lid on a going concern? Why stop? If you're worried about the new guv'nor, he's no problem; he's stopping nothing.'

From his pocket Matesa took the photograph taken by the Chinese photographer. 'Police. This face I know.'

Len Stevens squinted at the image. 'Yeah, I know this face, too...'

'It is in too many pictures. He is watching.'

'Is he?' Len came from behind the memorial to wave down the cemetery to his party, gave a thumbs-up as they nodded their appreciation of what they'd seen and heard. 'Nice one, Jack,' he called. 'You'll 'ave to come with me every trip...' He went back to give his attention to Matesa. 'Could be routine, he'll be all over the place, local plod, there's a lot of mugging, knives in the parks, drugs...'

Zlatko Matesa gripped Len's arm, hurt him. 'Tell them to buy him. Fix him.' He rubbed his thumb and fingers together signifying payment.

Len stared him in the eyes. 'He won't be any problem — but I'll tell 'em.'

Matesa nodded. 'Give me the money,' he said as he walked Len away, who handed over a bulky Jiffy bag from inside his mac.

'You don't need to count it, it's all there.'

'Same with the merchandise. But not today. I am holding back for one week.' With that Matesa stuffed the Jiffy bag into his top and walked back into the trees.

Len scowled after him. 'You what?'

'That was so special!' a woman came up to tell Len as he came back round the memorial. 'I'll never forget it...'

But Len Stevens only smiled weakly, as if he, too, had been affected in some way by what he had heard there that evening.

For four days and nights Song and the others slept and swayed, talked and sometimes quietly sang, ate bread or rice or cold salted horse meat, whatever the driver doled out to them at the overnight stops. Every muscle in Song's body ached with bracing and balancing in the back of the lorry, and when they stopped for the necessities and were allowed to clamber out, the road seemed to teeter and twist beneath her feet. Cramp, pins and needles, and the pain of clenching her insides until she could relieve herself, all made for hours at a time of great discomfort. Apart from quick daytime stops for himself only, Riz would pull up at night in some dust-driven lay-by where Song and the rest would hurry off into the rocks and sparse trees.

Lin was silent all the time now, driven deep within herself, clutching at her stomach as if her cramps were ten times worse than Song's. Song could do little for her, except cuddle her when she felt the girl's body shake with a sob.

At last, on the fourth evening, they were let out at a

smoking, a few lifting their heads towards the Chinese table as the food was brought, but no one taking much notice: this stop was part of Riz's routine, Song thought.

There was nothing any of the Chinese wouldn't eat: except Lin, who hardly ever ate much at all. The rest were very hungry, and Song found herself attacking a horse-meat sausage as if she bore it a grudge. Going into a new life would have to bring new things, and she was famished, but as she ate she remembered meals past in their Fuchow house, simple meals with poor food, but shared with her parents. The atmosphere in this café was calm and unstressed, and as her stomach filled, Song began to feel more like the ambitious Fang Song Yin again; sitting here at a table feeling civilized – the way she knew she would feel at her journey's end in England.

Until Riz returned from a visit outside: because when he came back he had another man with him, shorter, burlier, but wearing the same sort of astrakhan hat. Eating stopped; all the Chinese looked up. Who was this? Were they going to be handed on again? The man came over and bowed to the Chinese table, and before he sat to eat in another corner he walked around them, leaning over each of the party, shaking hands traditionally, hand and heart. He came to Song and bowed his head, staring her in the eyes as he shook her hand. But he held himself there for so long that Song started to feel uncomfortable, she didn't like this sort of attention; until he moved on, when everyone else seemed to get the same treatment. Perhaps it was the custom, Song thought.

The meal over, with a sudden squeal of his chair on the painted floor, Riz stood up. He clapped his hands. 'Now!' he said. Straight off, the atmosphere changed, from eating into a charged silence. Song caught her breath. Were the police outside? Had the café owner phoned them? Was this a trap, and Riz had to get them away fast? Or, could Riz be trusted at all?

Quickly, Song got up and crowded with the rest out through the door into the lorry park. But, 'Last chance!' Riz said. 'Toilet.' Song relaxed a little again; that was all it had been – the driver keeping to his timetable. Once more, the men went first, the accepted way now, to allow the women any privacy that was possible on the journey. Then it was a dash across the gravel to the lorry; the men urged in first, through the bales to the cramped quarters; the women following one by one. With his practised skill, Riz shut them in behind the heavy cotton bales; and within seconds the lorry juddered, and they were away, everyone falling into each other as they started to sort themselves to their places.

When, 'Fung!' the married man suddenly shouted. 'Where is Fung?'

Song squinted into the dim light.

'Where is Fung? My wife!'

Song looked about her, but there was nowhere much to look, only this cramped space. And Fung hadn't replied to her name. The married girl wasn't there.

'Tsai Fung!'

The lorry sped on. Fung's husband shouted, and Song and the others shouted for the driver to stop. The men clawed frantically at the bales, but there was no moving them, they were too tightly packed. There was no chance of being heard from the cab; there was no getting out; there was no going back.

It was Lao Zi who said it, the boy who had been cynical from the start. 'She was the prettiest,' he told them. 'Riz must have sold her to his friend, I saw the man give him something.' He shrugged. 'He's only a paid courier, Riz – that's his commission on the side...'

And from then on, it was not only Lin who was whimpering. After shouting his sworn threats till his throat was hoarse, Tsai Fung's husband fell to the floor of the lorry and cried his heart out.

Song sat upright and stared into the gloom of the lorry. What sort of song could ever mend such a broken spirit? What healing words could cover the wounds inflicted by a man who had seemed to be a friend, but who was a villain on the make? Hadn't Boss and the woman been more honest in their hardness?

And did jovial Uncle Chen know anything of these happenings?

Who in the world could be trusted any more?

Flo didn't say that she wouldn't be at the Regent's Arms on the Friday night. She didn't say much at all – and Ellie hadn't been able to bring herself to say anything to Flo either. But it would have been good if Flo had been there. There would have been a lot of making up to do, difficult explanations, but worth it if Ellie had a friend to turn to again, and a sort of accomplice on the lookout for the cigarette scam. But when Friday came, she wasn't there – although her mother was. Now Ellie had failed all round, because Mrs. Moses arrived just the same as before, down the steps with bags of food shortly after the music arrived – and she set herself up in the kitchen as if it really was hers tonight. When she saw Ellie she simply said, 'Flo! Flo! Don't ask me about Flo!' – as if she were washing her hands of a stubborn girl. But her face melted to a smile as Ellie's dad came over.

'Trying some new stuff tonight, Chrissie,' she told him. *Chrissie!* 'What we call inclusive catering – more chapattis an' some curried chicken for the baguettes. You get lots of different sorts in here.'

Chris Searle nodded. *Chrissie! That was what her*

mum had called him. And anything Mrs. Moses did seemed fine by him. So Ellie got out of it. She didn't offer to help in the kitchen, she didn't line up any glasses – but she wasn't going to sit alone in the bar all night in full view of Rude Boy Watson at his table by the door. She went off up to her room and lay on her bed in the foetal position, on her side with her legs tucked up to her chest. She had never felt so low since her mother's funeral. She'd thought she'd found a good friend, but the good friend's mother wanted to be an even better friend to her father. She'd thought a boy liked her as a girl, but he was only using her to go after someone else – never mind that she was using him, too. Her father was lining himself up for a spell in jail. And she had tried – and badly failed – to overcome her fear of water.

No good, no good, no good, no good. So what could she cling onto, to make her life worth living? Was there any part of her life that she could change, make a bit of success out of? Nothing!

She lay there on the bed, and in the way that the depressed do, she closed her eyes and slept. But it was a fitful sleep, not a night's sleep, there were tables and chairs being pushed about beneath her, and thumps as the stage went down and the speakers came in; until something shot her up on the bed.

It was a loud screech, piercing up through her

bedroom floor – feedback from a speaker as the microphone went live; to be quickly followed by the keyboard man saying sorry and the start of the recorded music that was always played before Ivy Stardust began her singing. Ellie knew the routine, she could picture what was going on down in the bar; but tonight it was different somehow, the music was louder, the bass seemed to run up the radiator pipe and shudder in her bedroom, a new sound from below – which could be coming from only one place: the large speaker that stood in the corner of the bar beneath her bedroom.

The large speaker that had never worked before – *because it had always come in filled with cigarettes.*

What was going on? Had she and Flo jumped to a conclusion too far? Was there no cigarette-smuggling scam after all? Ellie crammed her feet into her trainers and headed for her bedroom door. She hurried down the stairs and into the bar where the full sound suddenly hit her, where she had to find out what was going on; because whatever he'd said, her dad was going to be too busy behind the bar to do much snooping himself.

First she had to check that speaker, so she squeezed her way between the chairs – a smile here, a pat on her back there – and wriggled herself as close to the amp as she could get. Sitting nearest was a table of Asians – but none of Ivy Stardust's roadies who would have done the cigarette dealing were anywhere near. And sounding out from the speaker was Ivy's voice and the wire-brush and reed accompaniment from Len at the keyboard, a song about what a lovely way this was to spend an evening.

No!

Empty! The box had to be empty, apart from the blaster itself, or the sound couldn't come out as purely as it did. Ellie looked over towards her father, but he was busy behind the bar with a line of drinkers being quietly served; she looked past him towards the other big speaker that Flo had said didn't work, and through the door to the kitchen she caught Flo's mother's eye, she was filling baguettes with her curried chicken, which Ellie could have been helping with. Ellie looked away quickly, and stayed where she was. She couldn't make another move until the first song finished.

When it did, and as the customers clapped, a few of them moved – towards the drinks, towards the food – and there was just enough movement as Ivy Stardust took her applause for Ellie to do another quick series of sideways squeezes across the bar to the other side, where a table of real old East Enders sat by the other big speaker.

'You like our old music, love?'

'It's great!' Ellie nodded.

'Should've brought your bugle, Jack!' And the table nodded and didn't laugh.

The keyboard man improvised in the background while Ivy flicked through her folder of songs, picked one and told Len what was coming next. He ended a riff with a clever change of key, and off Ivy went into *The Lady is a Tramp*, one of her Ella Fitzgerald numbers – every word of which came out loud and clear through this other speaker. There were no cigarettes in this one, either.

There Ellie waited, out of everyone's way and out of Flo's mother's eyeline until the third song in the set was sung and Ivy Stardust had taken her applause and gone to sit at her table with her Watson party for a cigarette and a glass of Baileys which was ready waiting.

Now was the moment, then. If smuggled cigarettes were being sold in here, this was when it would happen. This was when people went near to the speakers and got served by one of Ivy's people, according to what she and Flo had thought. But, hard as she looked, there was no sign of it happening: not tonight. People moved about – to the bar, to the food, through the door to the outside – but Ellie could swear that no packets of two hundred passed hands, under, over or round the tables: Ivy's lot didn't even leave their seats.

So she went outside herself.

Tonight the canal was empty of vessels apart from the *Watson Travel* cabin cruiser, and those people who had come outside weren't standing and talking like before, flicking their cigarette butts into the water, they were drifting off, down towards the Basin, the other way towards Stepney Green Park, or round the Regent's Arms and up the steps to Salmon Lane.

So did that mean there was nothing more worth waiting for inside the pub tonight?

And there was no sign of the person who Ellie was especially looking out for – the policeman in plain clothes who had been keeping an eye on the place. It was a different night all round tonight.

She went back to the pub doorway. Ivy Stardust was starting her next set. The people in the room had more or less settled back, definitely a thinner crowd than before, and Ellie had a good view through to the bar – where her dad was still serving; but suddenly reaching through to him with a sandwich in her hand was Flo's mother: businesslike but caring, the way Ellie's mother would slide a coffee along the bar to him when he was pressed. Now he was busy so Flo's mother didn't linger, but as Ellie's dad turned from giving change to a customer, he saw her and gave her a slow wink, a split second longer than a *See you!* – which, to hold Ellie's breath, Madeleine Moses returned, with the slightest purse of her lips. Ellie's insides rolled at the sight. She still hadn't breathed and her mouth had gone dry as she fought to swallow the lump that had come in her throat. And standing there, leaning in the doorway, she knew why. It was jealousy. She knew jealousy, she was jealous of Flo for Jaz preferring her, she was jealous of Flo's mother for taking over her kitchen, and she was upset with her dad for having someone else besides her to smile at. And she realized, the truth of it coming to her so clearly standing here, that this was nothing to do with her mother dying, this jealousy wasn't for Jenny Searle, she wouldn't have denied her husband being happy – would she? This jealousy was Ellie Searle's for herself, for what the fact of her dad going with another woman meant to her, not to him, and not to her dead mother.

And still not moving, just breathing again, Ellie wondered – only wondered – if she shouldn't think the way her mother might have thought about her dad's well-being. Mightn't this be her dad's best chance for a new sort of happiness?

'You want a walk up the towpath?' Wayne Watson suddenly asked, coming round the door jamb. And he waggled his tongue at her.

'You oughta save that tongue for cleaning your shoe!' Ellie told him, before going inside, pushing through the middle of the singing, and taking herself off to where her evening had started, up to her bedroom.

To lie there wide awake while the evening wound itself down below her; but an hour and a half later to pretend to be asleep when a knock came on her bedroom door, and her father called, 'If you're awake – guess what? We sold some fags from the machine tonight!'

Which wouldn't be the only thing tonight that made you happy, Ellie thought.

If Riz had sold Tsai Fung to stuff his own vest with roubles, he got away with it. The lorry didn't stop until it had crossed the Russian border and arrived outside Astrakhan, Riz driving on and on, stopping only for the shortest relief, just for himself. There was just no getting at him.

At the beginning of this long run Song kept expecting them to be let out the same as before, even if one at a time; and Fung's husband crawled over to the bales with a knife in his mouth whenever the brakes went on. But they weren't let out – and as the hours went by Song could hold herself in no longer, and – the most humiliating thing – she started having to use the bucket, with no curtain and no screen, as well as enduring its disgusting smell. Her life back home had been poor, and simple; but her family had always kept its dignity, its respect for each other. Even when her father had been too ill to look after himself, things were done with love and tenderness, so that he wasn't distressed. How he would have hated to know what was happening to his daughter!

When, at long, foul, last the lorry stopped, the bales were pulled away to let the Chinese come tunnelling out, to the sight of two Russians with sawn-off shotguns aimed at the men – so that no one could move when they heard the driver's door slam.

They were counted, in Russian, and told 'nine' in English; as if the group had to agree with them; but neither of the Russians was prepared to listen to Tsai Fung's husband. Song looked around to see that she was in a narrow lane beside a single storey house amid fields of vegetables. It was something like home in Fuchow, except that these crops were growing healthily. With the rest she was waved towards the front of the house – until the Russians got close enough to smell the state of some of them and ushered them round to the side instead, where there was a tap beside a pigsty. Song waited her turn, and deliberately kept her parents out of her thoughts as – with no modesty left after the journey – she washed herself and her underwear under the run of the icy water. Layer by layer, Song seemed to be rubbing away the girl from Fuchow; she wasn't that person with spirit and dignity and a sense of joy any more, but a hardening traveller on a rocky road. And could she still sing, she wondered, or would that have gone, too?

Inside, the Russians kept hold of their guns – when, with a sudden door slam and engine rev, the cotton lorry drove away, too suddenly for Tsai Fung's husband to get out to it.

'Sit! He's gone!' one of the Russians said, putting down his gun. Now there was no more need for weapons: the Chinese depended on these men.

Neither of them ever gave their names, Song realized, not even using them with each other; just a chuck of the head and 'Vy!' in various tones. So she called one 'Bald-head' and the other 'Scar Arm' – the younger Russian being a pale, stubbly man of about thirty with a long knife scar down his left arm.

She was hungry now; but soon food was brought in by an elderly woman and given to Bald-head, who handed out cold pizza, everyone eating ferociously until Lin suddenly jumped up and ran outside to be sick, over the wall into the pigsty. Scar Arm followed her out, Song running quickly after.

'You don't like pizza?'

'Please, I am sick,' Lin told the man, clutching at her stomach.

'So the pig sees,' he replied, and laughed short and loud before taking the two back inside, where, as the darkness fell, Song squeezed with Lin into one of the cheap armchairs. But, exhausted as she was, Song couldn't sleep; too much had happened for her mind to be tranquil enough. She put an arm around Lin and murmured lullabies to the girl, who was crumpled like a sickly child. So what was the matter with her? What was her illness?

Song was still murmuring a nursery song quietly when, shortly after midnight, the sleepers were roused and they were all taken outside to a transit van. It just about held them, crowded into the back with the Russians, to be driven by the old woman to a place where Song could hear the shunting of a train. The van stopped, the Russians clambering out first and making the others wait; until, satisfied that there was no one about, they beckoned them to follow.

Song looked around her. They were at railway sidings. Immediately in front was a fence of old railway sleepers, which separated them from the shunting yard. Expertly, the Russians pivoted one of the sleepers aside and waved the Chinese through, across ballast and tracks to a long freight train of tarpaulined wagons.

Expertly, Scar Arm unlaced a few feet of the tarpaulin on a wagon near to the end of the train. Straight off, Song could smell the cargo. It was pine: timber, long trunks of it, with just room for people to squeeze together at the ends, where the lengths weren't all the same.

'Some this wagon, some the next,' Bald-head said.

'For how long?' one of the Chinese men asked.

He wasn't given a direct reply to that; instead, Scar

Arm reached inside his rucksack and pulled out a bottle
of vodka. 'Drink!' he said, taking a swig himself. 'Sleep,
dream happy!'

Some did drink, but Song didn't, she hated alcohol. It
was the men who were swigging – when a shout and a
scream suddenly turned all their heads. Lin was being
dragged back through the gap in the fence by Bald-head
and the old woman.

'Leave me! Let me stay here!' Lin was wailing. Song
was cross with herself: she hadn't seen the girl turn and
run off through the sleepers.

'Leave me! Let me go to a doctor, I am sick,' Lin
pleaded.

Some sighed, others moaned, this was happening
too much. They turned away and carried on dividing
themselves into groups for the two wagons. But Lao Zi
was swinging up his leg to go climbing into the space on
the first truck, when he turned back. 'She is not sick,' he
told them. 'I know her, she is from my village. I know her
husband, he is already in England – and she is having
his child.'

Lin broke into tears again, and Song took the arm of
the wretched girl. So that was it! Her husband had gone
to England and she was following him, carrying his baby.
Which was never allowed: Uncle Chen had asked Song a
question about that. But Lin was not a true seeker of a

new life, not the way that Song was: she could see it now. From the beginning she had been doing what she felt she had to, or what her husband had told her, not what she wanted to do. She should never have started this journey.

The two Russians looked at one another, and said something in their own language to the old woman. She shrugged – and they turned to Lin as if to manhandle her some more. But Song intervened. She took Lin's arm before they could, and walked her towards the back of the second wagon.

'Come on,' she said, 'there are better doctors in England, and good hospitals.' Watched by the scowling Russians, she helped the girl up onto the wagon, nothing else to be done, settling her as comfortably as she could. But as the old woman laced them and the older Russian tight under the tarpaulin, Song found herself wondering what the future really held for Hsaio-Yueh Lin.

CHAPTER NINE

Chris Searle came out of the Planning Department offices on the north side of Bow Road wearing the expression of someone who has had a fruitful meeting; copies of his papers and plans were in a black bag slung over his shoulder, and he patted it as he headed for his car. With some drawings he'd made and the notes of his needs that Madeleine Moses had helped him with, he'd outlined his plans to a borough planning officer.

She had listened attentively and asked some relevant questions – more to do with the change of usage from pub to restaurant than about the bricks and mortar of what needed to be done to the building. But in no way had the landlord of the Regent's Arms sensed Councillor Dot Bartram's community attitude. Here they worked with regulations not visions, everything had seemed very simple, and the officer – a young woman who had talked through the process very clearly, called him 'Chris' and not 'Mr. Searle' – had taken his plans and given him an application form to send to the council, either on paper or by e-mail. Nothing could have been more straightforward – and any idea that council officials had to tie you up in red tape had quickly been put out of Chris Searle's head.

He walked along Bow Road looking for the side street where his car was parked, managing to keep a straight face. He had mentioned Dot Bartram, to see if the name got a reaction, but the planning officer had said that most decisions of this sort were made by the officials, not the councillors – unless there was a problem and it went to committee. His eyes, therefore, had the glint of hope in them as he found his side street – until he saw Billy Watson standing by his car. Back to reality! Red tape isn't the only thing that can entangle.

'Thought I recognized the motor, guv'nor.'

'Ah. Didn't give it a shine for me, did you?' Chris

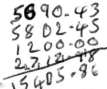

Searle stopped, and the joke died on his lips as from the doorway across the pavement Billy Watson's speaker men, his two heavyweights, came to stand alongside him.

Billy Watson wheezed. 'No, son, polishin' cars ain't my line of work.'

'Well, good to see you,' Chris said as he stepped into the road to go to the driver's door. 'What are you doing round here?'

'Hang on for a bit. I'm seein' you. I'm gonna buy you a drink.'

One of the big men came round to the off-side of the car to make it clear that Chris was not to get in.

'I can't have a drink. I'm a landlord, and I'm driving. Tonight, I'll see you tonight, won't I?'

But already the heavyweight was leaning in his leather jacket against the driver's door, his arms folded like a nightclub bouncer.

'Come on, we'll...' *wheeze and cough, and spit onto the pavement* '...have a word where it's quiet.'

Chris Searle looked all around him. The side street was empty, and a few metres away Bow Road was busy with trucks and vans, buses and cars, nobody giving a glance at four men by a Nissan Estate. It seemed there was nothing for it. He put his car keys into his pocket.

'I want to tell you about my Ivy,' Billy Watson said, as Chris was walked back into Bow Road and along to an old pub on the south side, the Cockney Bells. Inside, the place was empty – as empty as the Regent would be, back on the canal with Annie in charge. Here, the landlord, a whippet of an elderly Irishman in a striped shirt and balding hair slicked down in matching stripes, served them all with the coffees they asked for; except Billy, who made a big fuss over the great privilege of being made a pot of tea instead.

'What about Ivy?' Chris Searle asked – as the Irishman took himself away somewhere out of sight.

Billy Watson stirred his teapot while the others drank from heavy white mugs. 'It's mental,' he said.

'Mental?' Chris Searle put his mug down. 'How d'you mean?'

'I mean mental. Mental means mental. She's mental.' And Billy drank from his cup. 'Your business, guv'nor, your Friday nights is all that's keeping her with us – else she'd be inside somewhere. She lives for it, talks about nothing else, it's her therapy, standing up Friday nights an' being a star...'

'I thought she ran a travel business...'

'Yeah, but that runs itself. We've put in some good office sta...aa...ff –' interrupted by another rack in his throat.

Chris Searle tried to get this clarified. 'She seems all right to me, a good singer, knows what she's doing, always bright and...perky. You know, professional.' Chris looked at the other two men, who stared back at him.

'Oh, she'd be that. The pyschiactric sees all that. An' he sees the value of her Friday nights. Pre –' *cough and wheeze, and the lighting of a fresh cigarette...* ' –scribes them, if you like. Like I said, therapy.'

'Prescribes them?'

'Well, he says not to stop doing it, or she'll go downhill. Fast.'

Chris Searle put his coffee cup down and slid his shoulder bag round onto his lap.

'So, this is what I'm saying to you, guv'nor. If you pull the plug on Ivy's music nights, you put my wife into a mental home. Straight.'

Chris Searle stared at him. There wasn't the least moistness in Billy Watson's eyes that hadn't been there in the coughing. 'So you can see why I'm not taking kindly to any talk of you putting an end to things, exploring your other options.' Billy Watson looked down at the bag in Chris Searle's lap as if he knew what was in it.

The Regent's Arms landlord didn't nod, couldn't nod, he had frozen. And the bag in his lap with the planning application inside it lay there like a ticking time bomb.

'That's all. I've said all I'm gonna say. You get back to your pub, guv'nor.' Billy Watson stood up. 'An' we'll see you tonight. As per usual. Long as you understand...'

184

And he winked conspiratorially at Chris Searle as if Ivy were there and it all had to be behind her back.

That was it. Billy Watson walked with his men to the door of the pub, turned just once to shout over Chris Searle's head to the back of the bar. 'Ta, Roy!' And went out stamping on the pavement with the cough that racked him.

Chris Searle got up, turned to the publican, who was coming for the crockery whistling through his teeth: something that sounded like the theme from *The Godfather*. But the man wouldn't meet his eye as he rattled the mugs.

'Her? Ivy Stardust? Mentally ill?'

Coming in from school that Friday afternoon Ellie was shocked to see her father more dispirited than he'd ever looked since the death of her mother; and she thought she knew why. The council had given him the thumbs-down, it had to be that. Councillor Cake, as her dad called her, was obviously a powerful woman around here, and Ellie had been prepared for that – but not for this deep despair. Only when her father took her through to the kitchen and told her what had happened with Billy Watson did the full shocking reason for the dreadful sight of him become clear.

'I s'pose it could be mental illness, couldn't it?' he was saying in a thin, listless voice. 'You hear of some weird cases...'

Ellie sat at the table and thought about it. 'I s'pose it could be true.' Because Ellie knew that she acted normally enough herself to the outside world, but even her father didn't know the state she was in about water: she'd never admitted it to him. And her phobia was a form of mental illness, wasn't it? The fact that you know the cause of something doesn't make it any different in its effect. Some of the First World War stuff they were doing in history at school was about shell shock and battle fatigue; soldiers who became mentally ill, their officers knowing the reasons but still executing some of the men for cowardice – to set an example to the rest, to make them stay sane. It taught you that you had to show compassion when you could.

'Do you really believe Billy Watson?' Ellie asked. 'Or do you reckon it's a hook to hang their threats on?'

'Could be. She could get up and sing anywhere, couldn't she?'

'So if it is a racket, do you reckon your old Uncle Ronnie knew about what they were up to?'

Ellie's father shrugged, a sad shrug: some shrugs are quick and 'don't care' – this one was slow and 'no hope'. 'Then again, if they *are* up to anything,' he said.

'You didn't see anything last week, did you?'

Ellie shook her head. 'Well, is there any way you can do the both?' Always try to be positive. 'Run your smart restaurant the rest of the week but keep Ivy's singing nights on Fridays?'

Her dad looked at her, a face of grim, weathered sandstone. 'And end up in court, if there *is* something going on?' He sighed, a long, drawn-out end to his hopes and plans. 'Even if I didn't go to prison I'd lose my licence, an' this is my game.' His mournful eyes looked through to the empty bar.

'So we get our evidence and shop them!'

But the depressed can't be cheered up out of anything; they have to come out themselves. 'To get what? A fine? A couple of months? Would they get put away and never come back? No, not for shifting a few fags. And then what?'

Ellie shook her head at his pitiful croak of a voice; and she put her arms round his neck, and kissed him, and gave him as big a hug as she could manage. 'Then you ask someone about it. Privately. Try a policeman off duty, all hypothetical. Or Mrs. Moses. See what she reckons. She's a good one to talk to, isn't she?' And Ellie couldn't believe that she had just said that. It had just come out, the mouth overtaking the brain. What her dad needed right now was her mother, she'd always been good when things got tough – but she wasn't around any more, and off the top of her head Ellie couldn't think of anyone else.

But it had turned her father's head, lifted it slightly. 'Perhaps I will,' he said, 'if she comes tonight.'

'You don't know?' Ellie asked.

'I don't know anything any more,' he said, and went dejectedly back into the bar to relieve Annie, to give her time to go home and come back in the sparkly version.

And Ellie went upstairs to get ready herself; because she had just made up her mind – tonight she was going to be there for her dad, all evening.

That night there was no Flo again, but her mother came – and, unlike Annie, in a more subdued version tonight. She still looked great, but instead of gorgeous she looked beautiful; there were no bare shoulders and twinkling black beads on a shimmering dress, but a beautifully cut grey suit and a white silk blouse, the only colour coming from an amber necklace that shone in the lights. And she was early, before the music arrived. From her bedroom, Ellie saw her arriving and went downstairs, just to be about, so that Mrs. Moses wasn't the only one being nice to her dad tonight.

And it turned out that Ellie was why Mrs. Moses had

come in good time. Before she had unpacked her bags of food, before she had given Ellie's dad more than a first wave of hello, she had found Ellie – squirting and wiping down the kitchen surfaces – and she had come straight over to her.

'Poppet – is there somewhere we can talk? Quiet and private?'

Poppet? 'Sure,' Ellie said, and she led Mrs. Moses along through the bar and up to the first-floor sitting room that overlooked the canal. So what was this all about? Ellie sat her down in the grey-blue leather armchairs – her mother's choice – that they'd brought over from Charlton.

The woman had her eyes everywhere, she had never been up here before. 'Lovely suite,' Mrs. Moses said – but she didn't divert from her purpose. 'You, and me,' she began. 'You got a problem, Ellie?'

The chair that Ellie was in had never seemed so big; she was sitting on the edge of its seat like an infant in the Head's study. She didn't know whether to nod or shake her head to the question, or, like an infant, to stay there and say nothing, knowing that the adult is going to go on, regardless. But today had been a crucial one for Ellie; her father's state that afternoon had brought home to her that she had to make things right for him. Whatever she did right now, she had to play for the

Searle family team, and not her own selfish game. She shook her head.

'No problem? You sure?'

She shook it again.

'How about Flo? You got a problem with her?'

Once more, Ellie shook her head. And how she longed to put the clock back, not to have been the way she had, not to have put her own stupid self first. Would her dead mother have done something like she had done to a good friend? Jenny Searle had been a sharp partner in the pub, but in private life she had been the straightest person anyone could ever hope to meet.

'Flo says nothing to me, but I know she's all tangled up about you. One day she's talking twenty to the dozen about Ellie Searle, an' the next she's giving me the huffy shoulder if I even mention the Regent's Arms.'

Still Ellie could find no words that would come out sounding anything but stupid and selfish.

'I'll paint you my scenario,' Mrs. Moses said, her hands moving through the air in front of her, the imaginary canvas. 'You an' your dad, you're two on your own. He's told me about your mother, rest her soul, and the terrible circumstances.' She paused, and nodded her acknowledgment of them. 'Then along comes stupid, barging-in ol' Madeleine Moses, keen to find a new job local, an' in a week she's taking over the catering to

190

prove herself a good buy for anyone as wants a good chef. And the girl of the two, the daughter, she doesn't think it's right – probably not so soon – not appropriate for her dad to have much to do with some other woman.' She paused again. 'How wrong am I so far?'

Ellie stared across at her, the backs of her legs starting to sweat on the leather seat. She just managed a shake of her head.

'Then, what I've got to say is this...' Mrs. Moses was leaning forward, coming to her point. 'I like your dad, I like him very much. On our own the other day, we got on fine. We're both as ancient as Methuselah to you, but to us, we're not too old. No, not too old, an' this might develop, or it might not.' She flicked her hands out at the window to show how it might not. Now she lowered her voice, dead serious. 'But if you want me out, Poppet, if you want me away, if you don't want me to show my ugly face round this place ever again, you've only got to say so.'

Time froze in the still room, charged with protons. Ellie didn't know how you answered someone saying stuff like this; all she could do was sit silent, and squirm on the leather.

'I ain't coming between a girl and her dad. I ain't treading on any memories till due time – if it's one, two, or three years. But I've got a life, too, Ellie, and I've got my own loving daughter – the little minx-cat. An' you've got to be honest with me. Tell me now, or stop playin' any games. Welcome me in, or kick me out – an' you've got the last word on it, I promise. You say, an' I go.' Mrs. Moses got up, as if she were already on her way.

Ellie got up, too.

'So, you got anything to say to my speech?' Flo's mother asked. 'I hope I said it right, because I've been rehearsing it all day.'

Ellie wiped the backs of her legs with her hands. And she shook her head.

'You want time to think, to be sure?'

Mrs. Moses was very astute. Ellie nodded.

'But do I stay tonight, or do I go home?'

'Stay. Please.'

'Then come an' give us a hand with the provisions,' Mrs. Moses went on – and they walked downstairs together, each wrapped in their own silence.

The thirty-foot boat gave Song the nearest to comfort that she had had for two weeks. There were sleeping spaces for everyone, the Black Sea horizons were wide and other vessels could be seen from kilometres away, so she could lie on the deck sometimes, walk a few metres around it, and not be quietened if she gave a squeal when she slipped. And didn't she need some comfort after that splintering freight train, the choking cement lorry, and the long trek through more forest?

And she could sing sometimes – which was a relief, knowing that she still had the ability. She could stand in the aft of the boat, singing out to the water's wash. At first it was tentative, but as she grew in confidence and no one shouted at her, she began to raise her voice soprano high and sing to the emptiness: folk songs that her father had sung, and popular Peking opera that they'd heard on the radio at home. And with the ozone filling her lungs, she dared to think again of what lay at her journey's end: performances like this on a steady stage, and a sea of faces before her.

She never overdid it. Always, Song was aware of who she was, where she was, and what these people could be like, these men who did the trafficking. They still gave the orders, they still had to be obeyed, and a knife or a gun was never out of view. If they said something, the Chinese had to jump to it; one of them was always red-eyed on the lookout; and when they muttered to each other, there was always a fear of what they were saying in Russian. So Song made sure that she never went on so long that one or other would get fed up and shout at her to stop.

With the time to do it, though, Song persuaded Lin to

eat a little, and fed her with hopes for what England held for her and her unborn baby. Until the fourth night, with the Black Sea at its darkest and the cabin heavy with sleep – when with a jolt Song was roused by a creaking and a shaking of the bunk. She heard a stifled cry from Lin's bed below, and something growled low and sulphurous in Russian.

'What? What is it? What's going on?' Song tried to make out what was happening in the dark cabin, others waking now with cursing and questions.

'Some business. Go to sleep!' was all Bald-head said. 'No problem!' But there was a problem. A big problem: because right below her, Lin was being pulled roughly from her bed by Scar Arm, dragged out of it with a hand over her mouth, her arms pinned, her legs gripped tight by Bald-head – and was being carried squirming and twisting like a fighting fish out of the cabin.

Song rid herself of her blanket, jumped to the cabin floor, and, knocking herself against the bulkhead, raced towards the companionway. But the door was locked. She couldn't follow.

She thumped on the door – to the cussing of the cabin – but it wasn't opened, and it wouldn't give. All she could see was darkness, and all she could hear was Lin's screaming up on deck, a high loud screech like a creature at slaughter.

194

Which suddenly stopped. There was a loud splash, and then no more sound from Lin. Song went on thumping at the door. 'They've drowned her! They've drowned her!' she shouted to the fully roused cabin.

'She was fat with brat!' Lao Zi said. 'She was no good for trading, not with a kid. She was worthless to them!'

Lin's final scream had almost stopped Song's heart. She stood there, the boat still rocking from the energy of what had happened – they had thrown Lin from the boat into the deepest part of the Black Sea, where it made no difference any more whether she was a swimmer or not.

'I was her friend!' Song spat at Lao Zi. 'Her friend, her friend, her friend...' He didn't care – but what they had done to Lin had been cruel, heartless, ruthless! She had been like spoiled crop, and thrown away: and now Song knew that she was still here only because she could be sold on for good money. Her mouth tasted bitter, her throat hurt with its lump, her thumping heart seemed to want to explode. These men were not guides or couriers, they were gang members of a people business, and she herself was merchandise.

Now all she wanted was to be back in Fuchow, sleeping in her poor bed in the village where she had been someone loved, and not another person's property.

Her father had been a proud man, even when soldiers had come to Fuchow and given some of his fields to others. He had never been shackled by people or by a system. What would he think of his daughter being sold like this?

And what would Lin's mother ever think, if she one day heard of the wickedness of tonight?

CHAPTER TEN

No more was said about their conversation upstairs, Ellie and Mrs. Moses just worked like a team. The music had come in, heavy speakers – no doubt packed with cigarettes, Ellie reckoned – Ivy Stardust had appeared looking about as mentally ill as Boudicca, and the whole Watson outfit, especially Rude Boy, had swanned in through the door as arrogantly as cup winners. Now, in the kitchen, aprons over their Friday night outfits, Ellie and Mrs. Moses were into a routine. Slice, butter, pass across; slice, butter, pass across. And when Ellie got ahead of herself and passed across without buttering, Mrs. Moses said, 'Return to sender!' as she slid it back – and Ellie heard herself screech with a laugh like Flo's. But tonight, all at once, in the middle of one of Ivy's songs there was a sudden explosion of clapping and cheering, with shouts of 'Yes!' and the sound of chairs scuffing back as people stood. What was that all about? Ellie's head shot up as Ivy shouted, 'Thank you!' – and carried on with her song: and Ellie dashed to the kitchen door.

It wasn't clear, people had settled again, and Ivy was into a new verse of her song. But as she sang this slower number, a knowing smile on her face, Ellie found herself concentrating on the lyrics. And then she knew.

Ivy was singing a lovelorn song, about a lovely flame dying, and smoke getting in the eyes – underlined by suddenly pulling out from behind her back a long holder and a smoking cigarette. And there was the applause again, not so fierce this second time, but with loads of happy looks at one another as Ivy bowed, still singing, and gestured with an elegant arm around the room in a sort of invitation to them all.

Smoke! A cigarette! Ivy Stardust, on behalf of the Watson gang, had just announced to the audience that tonight it was business as usual! Ellie looked across to the bar, where her father was picking up the serving of a round of drinks, but catching her eye at the kitchen door. And he nodded. They were both thinking the same thing. There was no doubt.

Ivy finished the song and took her first break, over at her husband's table where a bottle of bubbly was being opened. But Ellie's eyes weren't on that for long. Hers were on the speakers now, and on the tables near them. Mrs. Moses was being as busy as the January sales at the kitchen counter, people milled around the bar as they always did, and tables of punters changed about. And among them, Ellie changed position, too. Unnoticed by anyone who might have cared, she slid her way to the nearest speaker, where one of the big guys was sitting at a table and serving. Not openly, of course, very much under the counter: but as Ellie watched, she saw the routine: people came to sit by him, gave him the raffle ticket that Rude Boy had sold them at the entrance, and in return – after a fumble behind – they were given plain, white carrier bags with something in them: which they put away in deep pockets or large handbags before they left the table.

Yes! It was happening, definitely. Something was being sold in here, what the people really came for was happening – the Watsons were back in their rotten business, pushing cigarettes. Pleasure hung in the pub air like a cup win.

Ellie quickly took the chance to double-check. 'Be back in a minute,' she told Mrs. Moses, and pushed her way through to the door and past where Rude Boy had folded his table away. Out on the towpath an elderly couple were heading for the steps up to Salmon Lane. And because they looked like genuine punters and not on anyone's payroll, Ellie took her chance.

'Get your fags all right?' she asked the woman.

'Yes, thank Gawd!' the woman said. 'Now he can have his little bit of pleasure without paying the chancellor!'

The old man looked as if nothing in this world could ever give him pleasure, but with her arm through his they went slowly up the steps, homeward. And now Ellie knew for certain. The Regent's Arms was definitely running a racket.

The evening went on in good spirits, and there was the same smug look when the Watsons went, at the end of what must have been a satisfying operation. They smiled, cracked jokes, hummed tunes, and carried out the speakers one-handed. And Ellie got a big hug from Ivy. 'Enjoy your night, love?' she asked. But she didn't wait for any reply.

'Well, we know for sure now about the Watsons,' Ellie told her father later. 'Because you saw what I saw when

had got the birds fluttering, it was who else was likely to be there. The policeman, doing his life-saving class.

It had been a jumpy start to the week all round. At school on the Monday Ellie had exposed her nerve endings to every hint from Flo's behaviour — because it was the first she'd seen of her since Mrs. Moses' request on the Friday night, and although Ellie wasn't ready to commit herself yet, she did wonder what might have been said back at Flo's flat. Perhaps Flo was going to come out with some terms of her own. So that week Ellie was half ready for a follow-up of some sort from the girl, and she twitched inside whenever Flo even moved her head. But after a couple of lessons the old pub daughter Ellie reasserted herself, and she put the Moses firmly in the problem box marked *Later*: being much more concerned with the threat to the Searles marked *Urgent*. It was the same on the Tuesday, but on the Wednesday, boxes with lids on or not, tough as she needed to be, her real fear of water still brought out the sweats — especially as it coincided with a new risky chance she'd decided to take.

The *Watson Travel* coach pulled up outside Limehouse High, with the same elderly driver as the week before, and Ellie's eyes wide open to connections with her other problem. And as she got into the coach, there it was, stuck up on a side window just behind the driver's head:

a small poster, slightly skewed. She read it as she slowed, going past.

BATTLEFIELD TOURS
First World War battlefields
and cemeteries of the Somme
Regular two day excursions
Ask driver for details

And Ellie bet that they did the Disneyland tours as well, which would mean that Watson's coaches made regular trips across to France: for old people, families, kids – definitely not the 'fags and booze' brigade whose vehicles were highly likely to be searched by police and customs. What a cover old people and kids would be for someone bringing in cigarettes from abroad! She had read about it on the internet, on the ASH website. Over a quarter of all cigarettes sold in Britain are smuggled, with others 'bootlegged' – where they're legally bought in places like France with a low tax on cigarettes, and brought to Britain where the tax hits the ceiling, one cigarette out of every twenty being smoked that way.

She sniffed about in her double seat like the child-catcher in *Chitty Chitty Bang Bang*, in case she might smell where tobacco had been, but it was obvious there was hardly anywhere suitable for smuggling in the coach saloon, unless packets went inside the seats, somehow. Also, this coach didn't have a toilet, so perhaps it didn't do the cross-Channel run itself, one of the others went. But as she got off the coach she had to make sure.

'These battlefield tours to France? Does this actual coach go?' she asked the driver.

The man eyed her but he answered with a nod. 'Believe it or not. Been round the clock a few times, this milometer.' And he smiled as he lit up a cigarette. 'But not me, girl, I'm British strictly left-hand side of the road meself. Let someone else go to Frogland!'

Ellie forced a smile and joined the rest on the pavement, ready to be led into the pool, but her eyes ran over the vehicle as it pulled away. Where could anything be stashed that wasn't meant to be found when it came through customs? All those lockers for luggage underneath, and the big boot at the back – they had to be searched from time to time. And when she thought about it, it didn't seem possible that the Watsons could get away with bringing in smuggled or bootlegged cigarettes time after time, regular. But as Ellie was going in through the doors of the pool and taking a last look back at the departing coach, something showed itself like a lump on a bald man's head. The air-conditioning unit on the roof of the coach. It was big, certainly looked too big for the coach, but wouldn't that do the job, wouldn't that hold a fair few cigarettes? On neither trip to the pool had the air vents in the coach wheezed out anything but London air with a bit of a cool blow to it, certainly nothing air-conditioned cold.

'Come on!'

And Ellie went into the pool, more certain and intent than ever in what she was going to do. But first she had to face her water phobia.

For someone who'd been as good a swimmer as Ellie once had, the beginners' lesson was the same mix of ability and fear as it had been before. The getting into the water – a dread, but doable when you've got the guts of Ellie Searle; the swimming – no problem hanging onto a float for a swimmer who'd once done her hundred metres; but the head under the water – that was the huge psychological barrier. Throughout the lesson, though, Ellie was buoyed up by a wild hope – because, like the week before, there at the other end of the pool was the police party doing their Bronze Medallion; and among them was the man she was determined to speak to, providing she could get to him before he went off to the changing rooms.

But the head under the water, that was the hang-up. When she stared down at it, it was as if the surface of that pool was clear poison, or a sheet of radioactive ice – no way could she go under it, especially for the stupid purpose of blowing out bubbles. Ellie's mother had blown out the last breath of her life in such bubbles.

They'd got to that moment where the line of beginners were at the bar, heads up to the instructor, whose eyes were fixed on Ellie as she told them, 'I know you enjoyed this bit before, it's easy, it's what gives the confidence to be real swimmers. It's faces under – remember? – and blow me some *real* loud bubbles this week!'

The others responded as if they'd been given a birthday treat – but Ellie, deep breaths, willing herself, eyes closed, eyes open, heart thumping, stomach churning, head light, down, up, nearly, no – again this week, she just couldn't force herself to do it. It was as if her shoulders and her head were in the grip of some strong restraining hand.

'Now, girl, you're going to do this for me, aren't you?' the instructor was asking her. 'You're not going to let these little ones see you fail. Just once, then you can have some free time for a play about...'

Why was it for *her*? Why did people say that? This wasn't for the instructor, it was for Ellie Searle! But free time afterwards, that was exactly what she wanted. She faced the water again. Down the line of children the bubbling was getting annoying. Enough! But Ellie closed her eyes, opened them again; took in a deep breath – and let it go. Failure. The line of tiles at the bottom of the pool eeled around, looked alive; but up here above the surface was life, and down there was death.

She shook her head. 'Can't.' And the angry thought suddenly hit her behind her welling eyes, why didn't the school have notes on her past — or if it did, why didn't the PE teachers read them? Why wasn't the system joined up enough for this halfwit on the side to know why she was frozen here?

'I want to get out,' Ellie told the woman.

'Oh, you can get out any time, love, if you want to give in.' The woman turned away and blew her whistle at the others. 'Free time!' she shouted. 'Well done, my brave fishes!' But now the instructor was there just for Ellie. 'Get out and go straight in to change — or blow me a little bubble.'

'Not to change,' Ellie pleaded. 'I can't do this, I can't, but I do need to get out.' She looked round to the deep end of the pool. 'My uncle's down there, with the police. If I say hello to him it might help me. Please.' It was pathetic, but it was a try, because Ellie was standing as fixed and rigid out of the water as a lighthouse; but angry — with herself, with the system, with the unfair world for putting her where she was.

The instructor looked to the other end of the pool. 'Oh, no,' she said. 'Not that first, then this. This first, then that. You can go down there when you've just put your face down onto the water, and a tiny millimetre under it, just for the time it takes to bubble me his name. Then up and you can go.'

Ellie looked round again. The policeman was still there, throwing the rubber brick into the water and jumping in after it. This was crucial – she couldn't go walking into the police station, it was in a busy street, and such visits were logged; she had to talk to him here, off the record. And today. The Watsons were up to their game again, and if her dad was counted in with them, he'd go to prison with the rest when it all came out. Ellie had to get in first with the police, and now was the perfect time.

'Yes?' The instructor was crouching above her, pretending to be kind; but she so wanted this notch on her tally stick. How Jenny Searle would have hated her!

And Ellie suddenly pictured her mother; not under the water in the bath – but storming into this swimming pool from whatever heaven she was in, anxious for the husband she'd left behind, but furious at the way her daughter was being treated. Ellie heard her angrily giving this instructor the mouth lashing she deserved, and hoicking Ellie up out of the pool and taking her to the far end, her dry arm round Ellie's wet shoulder, to talk to the police and put a stop to the criminality that was ruining her family's life.

And the spectre of her mother coming in there, the thought of the impossible that only a tough and angry south London mother could achieve, the memory of the dear, loved, strong person she'd been, somehow gave Ellie the push. Not the courage – this wasn't about courage, overcoming phobias isn't about being brave, it's about love and circumstance opening up a chance. But knowing that this was her crucial chance, doing it for her dad, Ellie faced down at the water, bent herself lower, and, telling herself that nothing was going to stop her going under there to kiss her mother's lips, she somehow – and suddenly – did what she had to. She put her face to the face of the water, and she bubbled. *I love you.*

'Splendid! There! Good girl! Now you can go and have a quick word with your uncle.'

God, Ellie wanted to pull that woman in and push *her* under. But, still shaking, she pulled herself up out of the water and padded along to the deep end – where 'her uncle' had just saved a drowning rubber brick by frog-kicking to the side on his back, clutching it to his chest. Ellie was shivering with cold – and with the thought of what, of whom, she had imagined just now.

She came up to the policeman.

'Yes? Want rescuing?'

'Definitely,' she chattered.

He was frowning. 'I know you from somewhere.'

'And I know you from somehow. Outside my dad's pub, the Regent's Arms, at the lock. Couple of Friday nights...'

'Ah.' With a quick look around he took her aside, away from the others. It was as if he didn't want any of the other police to know what was being said.

'Only, something's going on there – and I think I know what it is...'

'Do you?' In his trunks he didn't look like a policeman, now it seemed that he was trying not to sound like one, either. 'Is it something to do with...what goes up in smoke?' he asked her.

Ellie nodded.

'Then rest easy, because I know what it is, too...' He was looking cautiously back at the squad, though, as he said this.

'But you've got to know my dad's got nothing to do with it! And he's being threatened!' Now she'd done it. Now she'd done what the Watsons had warned her she shouldn't; what every blackmailer demands you shouldn't – and what the police always say you should. And she didn't like the attitude she was picking up from this policeman that he might be filing away her complaint. *Rest easy?* Was this copper bent? Had she put her dad in even greater danger by speaking out?

'I know he's not involved. *We* know he's not,' he corrected himself. And he lowered his voice, lowered his head to Ellie, to say, 'But you keep it to yourself, you hear? I want nothing out, not even that you've spoken to me, not even to your dad...'

'No?'

'I don't want a year's work scuppered, love,' he said. 'Schtum! Okay?'

Ellie nodded. 'If that's what you reckon.' Which suited her, too, if it wasn't going to have the police knocking on Billy Watson's door without enough evidence to prosecute: she and her dad could be the only losers if the police went off at half-cock.

'It is what I reckon,' he said. And without a word the policeman turned away and threw the rubber brick into the water again, letting it lie on the bottom before he jumped in to rescue it, and making one hell of a splash.

CHAPTER ELEVEN

Walking home from school, Ellie felt centimetres taller, and looking into shop windows at her reflection seemed to confirm it. So either she had grown since she last noticed, or she *was* walking taller — because of what had happened that day. It went over and over in her mind, as it had been doing since she'd dried and got dressed in the changing room. Dominating her thinking from back there in the shallow end was this strong sense that she had not been alone at the crucial moment, not when she needed someone, when it was succeed or fail. Okay, she didn't believe in ghosts – her sort didn't – but there had definitely been this weird feeling of a presence, of her mother's presence: which could have been a wish, could have been a memory, could even have been a spiritual contact with her soul; but all Ellie knew was that when she'd put her head under that water to kiss her mother's lips, she'd actually felt that that was what she was doing. The presence had been that real, and it had helped her to do what she thought she would never be able to do again. And now one of the first things she'd do when she got home would be to run a basin of water, and put her face under again: just to prove to the spirit of her mother watching her that she could, that Jen Searle still had an influence on her daughter. And also because she knew that she could do it.

And, regarding her father, hadn't she got the word of that policeman that things were in hand? Plus when things went down, when the Watsons went down, it would come from the police, not from the Searles: she and her dad wouldn't seem like grasses. So things were looking up, if she could trust the bloke: although that was a bigger 'if' than she'd really have liked. This cigarette scam had been going on for some time, so why hadn't he done something about it before now? But overall there was a bit of hope, although she mustn't say anything about it to her father, not yet. Who knew, though, that day when he could live his dream and convert the Regent into a smart little canal-side restaurant might not be all that far off. Yes, she decided, all ends up she was definitely walking a bit taller than before...

The afternoon BAe146 jet came into London City Airport, descending at its steep angle to use three-quarters of the runway before turning and taxiing to the arrivals lounge. The plane from Paris was filled with city business people, but it had been from choice that loner Zlatko Matesa had booked seat 21C, the one on its own at the back. 'What line are you in?' was a question he would never be asked by a nosy traveller.

Once inside the black cab with the Chinese photographer who had met him, all he said was, 'Watson. You take me to Watson.'

'It's fixed,' she said. 'He'll meet you where he isn't known.' And she handed him something that he put in his coat pocket.

'This is where?'

'St Paul's Cathedral,' the girl instructed through the interior window. But seeing the microphone that linked them to the driver, Matesa said nothing to that – and no more at all until the cab had been paid off in Paternoster Row and they were walking up the broad steps to the famous Wren building. 'So he hides under the hand of God!'

It was busy inside with tourists, and with the boys of the cathedral choir beautifully rehearsing their part in a Mozart requiem for the dead.

Matesa's eyes widened in the change of light and he looked about. 'He is where?' he wanted to know, reaching for a cigarette, then cancelling the move with a frustrated click in his throat.

'He is in a small place where people pray...'

'It is good that he prays. This meeting should not have to be.'

Watson was in a chapel off the north aisle, and Matesa and the girl slid into the pew beside him, facing an ornate altar. The East End businessman didn't look up, or round, but continued staring at his feet, although the tightening of the cloth across the back of his jacket said that he knew who was there.

'Out!' Matesa told the girl. 'You, outside!' He jerked his head.

The girl went.

Now Billy Watson stood up. 'And us, an' all,' he said to Matesa, 'we can't talk in here...'

'You say this place.'

'For the meet. Easy to find. For talking, we go outside, there's a pub handy, or a caff...'

Billy Watson was standing, Matesa still sitting. Suddenly, Matesa grabbed Watson's arm and sat him down again. 'Is not me dancing Watson's dance, is Watson dancing mine! I come to say you one thing –'

As he spoke, he put his hand into his pocket, and brought out a twelve-centimetre long metal cylinder, which he twisted round and round in his fingers like an executive stress toy. 'So you listen.'

Billy Watson knew what the object was, and listened, hard. It was the silencer from a nine millimetre pistol. He sat very still. 'What you got to say?'

Matesa looked around, stared at the verger, who moved on. 'You are this small fish,' he hissed at the back of Watson's neck. 'Matesa is bigger fish, and others are bigger than Matesa. Lot bigger, in China, Russia, England.'

'We only try to play our part,' Billy Watson wheezed. 'We give you cover, where else are you going to find what we give? You want busy-busy, we give you busy-busy.'

'And busy*body*? That how you say it? That police?'

Billy Watson shuffled on the pew. 'Yeah, Len told me you reckon you seen him, in some photograph, but he's no bother, I swear.'

'I know him from before, he arrests me for running small racket, he knows me. I don't like him so close...'

'Which is why you're off the scene, in France – am I right? But I'm saying, he's no bother to us. He's around, yes, because he's local Old Bill. An' local means he's about the place local, don't it? O' course your photographer girl's gonna see him around. But he's no trouble, on my mother's eyes...'

'And this new man at the Regent? He is no trouble? Everything is still good?'

'Diamond. He's diamond. He knows which side his bread's buttered.'

Zlatko Matesa stared at him, then put the silencer back into his pocket and, pulling out his empty hand, cupped it, thrust it under Watson's nose. 'Both, they are in there? Him and police?'

Billy Watson looked down at the hand; then he slowly folded Matesa's fingers closed. 'Tight. No problem,' he said. 'No problem.'

Matesa kept his fingers closed before suddenly making a fist of the hand and bringing it up under Billy Watson's chin, forcing it against his Adam's apple.

'People running me, running you, they will kill if you tell me lies. No, *I* will kill!' He patted his pocket. 'This I will use!' He pushed his fist tighter into Billy Watson's throat. 'This is biggest business!'

He took the pressure off the man's throat, got up, and walked towards the huge west door of the cathedral, grabbing at his pocket for a cigarette as he went. To the strains of the boys singing Mozart:

When the judge takes his place,
what is hidden will be revealed,
nothing will remain unavenged.

And Billy Watson started breathing, and coughing, again.

Dominoes. One domino is pushed and the push is passed on. So it was with Billy Watson. Ten minutes ahead of Ellie getting in from school, Chris Searle was having a visit — from Watson's two strongmen. They banged into the empty pub and one of them marched to the bar, thumping a fist for attention. The other stood like a bouncer in the doorway.

Chris Searle came out from some paperwork in the small office at the bar end. 'Yes?' he asked, suddenly going the colour of the kitchen wall — and moving himself to where he was in reach of the baseball bat he always kept behind the bar.

'Just to check, *guv'nor*' — said with a sneer — 'you did remember what Mr. Watson told you about his Ivy? You did cotton on how the Friday nights 'aven't got to stop?'

'I heard what he said, yes.'

'But did you listen real hard, take it in?'

'I reckon so.'

'Well, I'll make it plain as that nose on your face, 'cos he's too much of a gentleman to use strong language.' Suddenly, from nowhere, the man grabbed Chris's wrist, and with his other hand he whipped a fishing knife up from under his leather jacket and held its point at Chris's left eye. 'An' you move for that club under there an' I stab you blind!'

Chris dare not nod: the point of the blade was a millimetre from his eyeball.

'Now hear me good, right? Them papers you've got in with the council – you take 'em back. You go an' tell the council you've made a mistake. This place is for music Fridays, okay, none of your other poncy plans. You shoot them ideas down the lav.' Chris's wrist was jerked, some reply needed. 'Uh?'

'Is this from Billy Watson?' Chris got out.

His question was ignored. 'You don't say nothing to your girl, you don't say nothing to no one essept the council, right? An' you don't say nothing to no police! You just do the business like I said. Uh?'

'No app...lication.'

'Or, not you – but it's the girl who'll cop it. She'll be the accident in the canal. You understand?'

Chris said, 'Yes,' loudly. He understood.

'Okay.' The man took the knife away from Chris's face. 'Oh, yeah, and Mr. Watson sends you his best.' Then he turned and went, walked out and away, followed by the other one – just a few moments before Ellie came home to the Regent's Arms from the opposite direction.

To where her dad was all smiles: so falsely smiley that she had to wonder what he was up to.

'You been out to lunch?' she asked him.

'No, love. Why?'

'Not a business meeting with Mrs. Moses?'

'Do I look like that?'

'I dunno what that looks like, just, you're all 'up' about something...'

'No, love – only the thought of a run to the cash 'n' carry, that's all...'

Ellie groaned. 'Oh, is this the night?' How back-to-earth was that? Does an Olympic swimmer win two golds then shoot down to Asda?

'When you're ready, after Annie comes.'

And now Ellie was in a new muddle. She still felt happy with herself; going up the stairs with her school bag, pulling out her wet costume as she went past the bathroom with some sense of achievement; and she still reckoned that she'd done the right thing in speaking to that policeman. But she was definitely puzzled by her father's pale face and that weird sense of agitation he had about him. So what was he up to? What was his game?

And there *was* something going on, no doubt – judging by how poorly he drove the car that evening, not seeing others, even crossing a light at red.

'Watch out!' said Ellie, as the hooting told him what a stupid driver he was, going on to park across two spaces in the cash 'n' carry car park. Fortunately there was plenty of room; it was always a good day and time to go because it wasn't too busy, outside or in. The aisles were clearer, you could see people coming, you weren't likely to be caught by surprise by someone. And Ellie was always on the lookout for Jaz Prabhaker – even though she guessed his mother wouldn't be wanting a new television every week. That boy she didn't want to meet anywhere out of school.

But they met someone else inside, coming round a blind corner pushing a long, empty trolley. The music man, keyboards Len.

'Well, blow me!' he said. 'Small world.'

'Yeah,' said Chris Searle. 'Got to keep my Friday punters happy...'

What was all this? Ellie asked herself. *Sucking up to this man about Fridays!*

'Sure,' Len said, 'you need to do that,' and pushed his long trolley another way.

Weirdly, though, when he got to the checkout in a next-door-but-one queue, all he had on his long trolley was a pack of blank recordable CDs, looking like a brick on the back of a lorry.

'Not in for your usual?' the supervisor asked him as she stamped his invoice and let him out.

'Ain't got what I want,' he told her in a low voice, hurrying off.

But he wasn't Ellie's concern. Her father was: he wasn't being Chris Searle; suddenly tonight he was someone else.

What was going on? It had been a false face put on for her, Ellie knew that. No, it wasn't him, but she had seen it once before and it had squirmed her then as it squirmed her now. It was when he pulled out his bright smiles on the day he was let go by Gillingham Football Club, with a choice between playing in a lower league, or leaving football altogether. A mouthful of grinning teeth then, he had pretended that that had been just what he wanted, a modest testimonial match to send him on his way into a new life in pub management. But Ellie's mum had known better, and so had Ellie. Young as she was at the time, Ellie knew that the biggest hurt to a professional footballer comes when he's reckoned to be over the top and not worth the wages. And Gillingham was no Manchester United. She had cried herself to sleep that night for her dad, because his bright smile had been one of the most pathetic looks she had ever seen on anyone's face.

Things were that bad again now. Or worse. He'd been threatened by the Watsons, she knew that, because she'd been threatened, too. And today they'd upped things a gear, they must have done. Something had happened while she was at school that her dad was trying to cover up.

She lay on her bed and stared up at the design on her lampshade, eyes wide, sighing on every other breath. The other night she'd seen the brightest, most genuine smile she'd seen from her dad in ages, given to Mrs. Moses, while by making bad friends with the woman's daughter she'd be wiping off that smile.

So what sort of a slug was Ellie Searle to deny her dad the one bit of happiness he was likely to get? How *selfish* was she? And despite her own pleasure at what had happened at the pool, in spite – or because of – the spirit of a dead mother who loved both of them still, did she ever want to see that Gillingham smile on her dad's face again?

And the answer to that was 'no': and riding with it was another answer – to the question of what to do about it, of how Ellie could help to make things better. It was obvious. She had been so selfish. Now she *had* to give her dad the chance of a new life: and that would mean a change of direction. She had already made up her mind to do it; so now she had to see that she did, and a darned sight sooner than later.

Ellie's change of direction was one hundred and eighty degrees, to the person sitting next to her in class on the Wednesday morning: straight to Flo Moses. The girl had come into the form room from her mates in the yard the same as usual, no particular aggravation, but no warmth – just neutral, like another passenger sitting next to Ellie on a bus. But with the class waiting for a late teacher, talking, whooping, disgorging bags, two boys fighting with the flappy arms of their coats, there was a chance to talk. Ellie had been hoping for it sometime soon, and she took it.

'What do you call a chicken that's crossed the wrong road?' she suddenly asked Flo.

'Ellie Searle,' Flo answered without looking round – the answer Ellie was going to give after the next clue: *a daft chicken that couldn't see straight?* The oil had just been sucked from the works.

'Dead right,' Ellie picked up. 'And I've got no excuse for it except being selfish, which isn't any excuse, I know that, and I can only—'

But Flo had swung round to face her, millimetres between their noses. 'My mum brought this up?' she asked. 'Is this you talking to me, or your dad?'

Ellie stared back, willed her eyes not to make her blink till she'd got one sentence out. 'Your mum,' she said, as dry in the mouth as brick dust. 'Friday night; and, no, not my dad talking – just me.' Now she had to blink, probably because she'd so not wanted to. 'Your mum gave me the option – and...it made me see what an idiot I've been.'

Flo hadn't blinked, though. She went on staring, not a hint of an expression on her face. 'Took you a long time, then, didn't it? Friday, Saturday, Sunday, Monday, Tuesday, Wednesday...'

'I know. It's because my mum's not been dead that long...' This conversation had gone well off the rails of Ellie's planning. There was a long silence between them.

'Why do you think I let you sit here?' Flo broke it. 'Why do you think I haven't made your life so rotten you'd want to throw yourself in your stinking canal? Why have—'

Ellie was shaking her head; she had to make a pacifying gesture of some sort – a lot more than Ellie Searle hung on this. Except, it was wasted. Before Flo could finish her next *Why?* they were interrupted by Ms. Religious Education coming in from the staff room looking like she'd got in late from a rough night. Mouths and bags zipped up, the fighting sleeves dropped dead over the seat backs, and Flo faced front again.

Nothing sorted.

Off the Bow Road, Chris Searle was at the council offices. It was a short visit, made easier by being dealt with by the same woman as before. She remembered his application well.

'Has this been seen by any councillors yet?' he asked her. 'Dot Bartram or anyone?'

'I told you, Mr. Searle, this will be dealt with in the office. Only if there's a problem or a controversial proposal does it go to council members.'

'Well, I'd like to have it back, please,' Chris told her. 'I want to look at it again.'

'To modify it?'

'No.' There was a very long pause. 'Probably to cancel it...'

'Altogether?'

'It hasn't gone anywhere yet, has it?'

'No. It's on my desk in the other office, waiting for the application form I gave you.'

'Then could I have it back, please?'

The woman looked at him as if she might say something about wasting council time, but she had been polite and helpful before and she was the same again. 'Here,' she said, bringing it.

He took it; it was still in the envelope with his hopeful

handwriting on the front, but when he slid it out he saw that the plans had a council stamp on the first page, showing the date they had been submitted. The woman got up to go, but Chris stayed seated.

'Could you do me one more favour?' he asked her. 'Could you write "withdrawn" on this – and sign it?'

The woman thought for a moment whether or not this was within her remit. But she smiled and did so. 'This looked exciting. It must be a disappointment for you. Was it the money?' she asked. 'It was quite ambitious.'

'Something like that,' Chris told her. And, 'More than a disappointment, as it goes,' he said as he went.

Time and darkness play strange tricks. How long had Song been a prisoner in the container? Only her bladder kept time for her, and judging by her blind visits to the bucket at the far end of the space, it was four or five hours perhaps.

They shared the space with a mothballed car, everything Song bumped against hard-sided – unlike the Italian plant lorry from Tuscany that had disappointingly taken another route. Filled with cypress trees and wisteria, it had been soft and fragrant, and its canvas walls had given a kind of light inside. But there was no comfort in this claustrophobic container. Romania, Hungary, Austria, Germany, she had climbed over many tailboards, hidden with many cargos, slept in a succession of barns, fields, warehouse cellars and cheap hotels. This was different, though; this total blackness with the limited amount of air that had been sealed in with them when the back was slammed shut – ages before. They were in France, she knew that, and getting nearer to England; but she couldn't wait for this part of the journey to end.

At one point, after the continuous rumble of the wheels, the container lorry did come to a stop; before suddenly starting again and beginning to twist and turn, stopping and starting – seeming to have come off an autoroute and driven into a town.

So were they near to the driver's delivery point – or to where the Russians were making him take them? Song held fast to the charm round her neck as others in the container tried to guess.

'We're there! Getting near somewhere!'

'Near docks?'

'Who knows? But, please, don't let us be lifted! When we stop, please not onto a stack!'

The lorry did stop, and when it didn't start again quickly, every breath was held. What would happen next? Would they be let out – or would they be abandoned to die in here until the mothballed car finally reached its dealer? Was this to be the start of a long, suffering death? No one wanted to put voice to it; and when Lao Zi began to say something in his sneering voice, he was told to shut up.

But at last they heard the muffled slam of doors; followed, mercifully, by the rattling sounds of the container being opened. Song waited with the rest, eyes trying to pierce the dark as the doors opened a crack and light crept timidly in, then flooded, bright, white, blinding; daylight; sunshine; and with it came a waft of fresh, autumn air. Song closed her eyes and breathed it in as she had never breathed anything in her life. She was coming out of the container! Thank you, little peach!

Squinting her eyes, she saw a long avenue of trees stretching before her, and a white minibus stopped only metres away on the road.

'Quick!' shouted a man standing there. 'In here!' He ushered, hurried, pushed Song and the others to be quick into the smaller vehicle. Of the Russians Song saw no sign at first – although a scarred arm, resting on an open window, said that they were still up there in the container cab, still frightening and ruling its driver.

Song found a seat quickly, and with a foul word and a sliding slam of the door, the man who had met them

jumped into the driver's seat, and they were off —
speeding along the avenue, where a road sign told Song
that they were passing through a place called Verdun.

Her life now in the hands of this man who was
smoking a foul, yellow cigarette as he drove.

CHAPTER TWELVE

The *Laughing Lady* lay ready at Corbie as the French narrowboat *Hélène* came north up the Canal de la Somme and moored alongside. The bumpers were in place, Ken the young Chinese deckhand running around on his toes, and Hector McLeish standing like a threat on the bridge, the engines idling. Just above water level the pumps were puttering water out into the canal as Zlatko Matesa climbed the short ladder aft.

'We're ready,' McLeish said, coming out onto deck. 'Dark. Wait for dark.'

Matesa took a good look around the Corbie landscape through a pair of night-vision binoculars, McLeish seeming to stand to attention until he had finished.

'No problem,' Matesa said, flicking a cigarette butt into the water, the signal to transfer the cargo from one vessel to the other.

When the transfer was over he thumped the side of the cabin cruiser like someone despatching a taxi. 'Nine!' he said, and he had disappeared into the *Héléne*'s stuffy cabin before Hector McLeish had opened up his engines.

The rest of that day was frustrating for Ellie. Now she didn't know where she stood – or sat. At break time Flo found her other friends as she'd been doing since the Jaz Prabhaker business; and Ellie – who had hoped to be back on better terms with her – hovered in the doorway for an invitation to join them, but none came. Jaz Prabhaker came in with his arm around the shoulders of a Year Eight girl, ignoring Ellie as if she were one of the canteen pillars; and nothing was new. Wayne Watson was loud and rude with a pack of dirty playing cards near the drinks machine, so Ellie wouldn't go there, and in the end she did what she'd been doing most days for a couple of weeks, she pushed out of the canteen and went to sit at a computer screen in the library. At least she'd been getting more homework done on school premises. But she had said her piece to Flo and there wasn't much more she could do now but wait to see what happened.

The *Laughing Lady* was having a rough crossing. The October wind from the south-west was whipping up the Channel, and crossing the dangerous shipping lanes meant that Hector McLeish had his work cut out manoeuvring between other vessels and keeping the swell running with him, not across him. Both he and his wife were good sailors but the deckhand wasn't; he was a wretched, retching sight on the aft deck; and for Song and the rest in the cabin the Black Sea had seemed like a boating lake compared with this.

From the container lorry they had been taken by minibus to Château Renoir-sur-Marne, and after two nights of staying quiet in Matesa's dirty little house – not too much trouble for Song because she had slept and slept – they had been driven to a marina in the early hours of the next day, where they were put upon a narrowboat on the Marne and through to the Canal de la Somme. From there it had been this boat, and the English Channel, and no fresh sea air to breathe however sick they felt.

At last, near the English coast, the sea calmed – when there was a sudden shout down from the wheelhouse – 'Coastguard!' – and the captain's wife leaped to pull aside a rug, exposing the trapdoor hatchway in the planks of the floor that they'd been shown before.

'Down! Hurry up! Quick!' Myra McLeish shouted, and with the rest, Song was pushed down headfirst to wriggle inside the foul-smelling bilge, that lowest part of the boat where water and oil swills about, despite a pump continually running, the first of them pushed to go on further inside the claustrophobic space – where all that any of them could do was lie there staying as silent as the grave, the decking of the cabin only inches above their heads.

Now, despite everything that had gone before, Song's pulse ran faster, her blood seemed thinner, as the crucial part of the long journey began – the illegal entry into England. *But what was this all about?* she asked herself, lying there trying not to choke on the oily water. With England in sight, Uncle Chen had promised no trouble, no danger. This was as bad as that container lorry – worse!

'Ahoy, Hector!' sang the coastguard above.

'Ahoy, yeself!' Hector McLeish greeted warmly as the cutter came alongside.

'How's it going, you Scotch mist?' Jack Williams shouted into the breeze.

'Fair to middling...' The conversation was up-and-down as the swell ran under both vessels. 'You're coming aboard for a dram?'

'Just to settle the stomach,' said the Watch Officer, who even in his oilskins was youngish, slim and fit. 'Hold off there, Jim,' he shouted behind him as he jumped with ease for the *Laughing Lady* ladder and climbed it. The glasses of straight single malt whisky were already poured as he came in through the wheelhouse door. 'Cheers. So, was it undiluted pleasure, this trip, or a spot of business as well?'

'Oh, y'know me, Jack. I'm not for running these great engines for the sake of the wife back in the cabin. A wee break, fine, but it's got to pay for itself, every time.'

'I guess so. But I'd better take a look, just to say I've done my duty when they smell the drink on my breath.' The coastguard laughed, knocked back his drink and went down through the internal door to the cabin: where, at the far end in the dinette galley, Myra McLeish was filling a pan, to make a start on a meal now that the sea was calmer.

'Jack! Ye've come back to see me.' She had the radio turned up loud to music from BBC Radio Kent, but shouted at Jack rather than turning it down.

'Myra. So, what have you got today?'

'Put a few tatties inside us,' she said. 'And stir-fry chicken for the boy, if he can keep it down.'

They both laughed as Jack Williams's eyes surveyed the cabin, from the carpeted deck to the swinging ceiling lamps, from the cushioned port side lockers to the starboard. 'Very nice — but what I meant was, what cargo? Hector says he's not neglected business on his wee holiday...'

'You can lay a pension on that!' Myra McLeish eyed him, and set her pan in the sink where it wouldn't tumble. 'A St Katherine's Dock wedding, Saturday week. Royal guests!' She went to the starboard side locker, pushed the cushions aside and opened it. 'Champagne from Etoges, if it hasn't all popped off in that Channel weather!'

Jack Williams looked. Twenty cases of Borel-Lucas were stacked neatly within the locker, with a 'duty-paid' invoice stapled to one on the top, which the coastguard scrutinized carefully.

'Open up a case,' Myra invited. 'Be sure.'

'Oh, I'm sure.' Jack Williams shut the locker top and replaced the cushions himself; then his eye went to the port locker on the other side of the cabin. 'And surely something for yourselves?'

'As if!' Myra laughed. 'Right enough — Bordeaux, wouldn't you think?' She threw the cushions off the second locker and opened its top; and here were a dozen cases of a good claret; again, with a customs and excise 'duty-paid' invoice, stamped at St Valery.

'All fine an' dandy,' Jack Williams said. Again, he reassembled the cushions — where a scrap of paper fluttered to the floor. He picked it up. It was a sheet from a notepad, covered with Chinese writing in ballpoint pen.

'The boy's!' Myra McLeish laughed. 'Ken! Homework! Still trying to read and write in his own language!'

'He's in a bad way right now,' the coastguard said.

'He'll have to get used to it if he's going to go on working for us,' Myra told him. 'We can't heave-to for a wee drop of bad weather.'

'Me neither, Myra,' Jack Williams replied. 'It goes with the wet, eh?'

And within a few minutes he was back on deck, signalling the cutter to come alongside to take him off. But before his vessel was out of sight, Hector McLeish was clinking glasses with Myra up in the wheelhouse.

'Here's tae a drap o' villainy!' he said.

'Should I let them out just now?' she asked him, pointing down to the bilges.

'Drink your whisky. They'll be fine for a wee while longer...'

* * *

Song had never been in such a terrifying, confined space, down between the cabin floor and the boat's hull. The container lorry had been like the open fields compared with this. Her back, her legs and her hair were drenched with foul-smelling bilge, she cracked her head on the decking above her whenever the boat dipped into a trough, and she was so tightly packed that she couldn't move an arm to clear her mouth when the bilge lapped over her face.

No, this was no private yacht into England, the way that Uncle Chen had described it. And nothing much else had been as Uncle Chen had described it. All these snakehead people, from Nanjing to this boat, were bullies and killers, who treated the Chinese worse than goats and chickens in Fuchow market: bought and sold – and put down, if necessary!

Another slop of filthy bilge filled her ears before it choked into her mouth, and she hit her head again as her body coughed it out. The engine throbbed through her body, and her claustrophobic inside wanted to shout to be let out, racked with the thought of what her mother's face would look like, if she saw her daughter now...

It was Thursday afternoon, and still nothing definite had come from Flo – except that during the day she had shared their classwork with a touch more closeness, acted just a few degrees warmer. She actually made an 'Ellie' joke in class. When the geography teacher asked a question about the points of the compass, wanting to know the difference in degrees between east-south-east and south-east, Flo called out, 'Ellie knows; she's from the sarf east...' But it was 'Ellie', not 'Ellie Searle', and neither the remark or the laugh were unfriendly. There hadn't been anything else, though, and what remained a mystery for the rest of the week was what had stopped Flo from taking some nasty action against her.

But now, as Ellie came in from school and shared a cup of tea with her dad, she thought home thoughts – and she suddenly put her hand across the kitchen table and stroked his. It was cold.

'All I want is for you to be happy,' she told him. 'And shall I tell you one reason to help you be happy? Cheer you up?'

'Go on,' he said, looking surprised, but a long way from eager to hear.

'Swimming. Tuesday. Do you know what I did at the pool?'

'You never peed in the water?'

'No!'

'Did your four-hundred metres? Do we need wall space for a certificate?'

'*No!*' The man didn't even know why she was attending the pool. She took in a breath. 'I put my head underwater!'

Her father frowned. 'I didn't know you couldn't,' he said.

Ellie stared at him. 'Well, I couldn't for a while,' she said. 'And now I can.'

'Well done.'

But if she'd been going to say any more, about her mum, or about talking to the policeman — which she hadn't planned to, except sometimes she never knew where she'd end up — she didn't, she kept her mouth shut. Instead, she got up and started rinsing her cup in the sink. Her dad was in no receptive mood. 'I'll clear the decks for Mrs. Moses, tomorrow,' she told him. 'She is coming, is she?' She took a sneaky look over her shoulder at him; because this was a sixty-four million dollar question, twice over.

'As far as I know.'

'Well, if she isn't, we've got no food in. Have you rung her? And if you haven't rung her, have you got plans to get stuff? Or that means no food tomorrow night. At least I'll know what I'm *not* doing!'

Chris Searle sat over his cup of tea with a small, wistful look on his face. He was still so pathetic; and without planning to, Ellie suddenly came out with it. She shut the kitchen door, sat herself down again, and took both her father's hands in hers. 'I've got a bit of news for you – because like I said, I only want you to be happy,' she told him.

'I doubt if I'll ever be happy again,' he interrupted, a glisten to his eyes. 'Ellie, it's all gone so wrong...'

'No it hasn't, not all of it.'

'Do you know what I did today?' he asked her, staring into her eyes. 'I tore up my application for planning permission...'

Ellie straightened. 'You did *what*?' That was a stroke she hadn't anticipated. Was that why he'd been looking so different? 'Who was that down to? Dot Bartram – Councillor Cake? Or who? Who brought that on?'

'No one. Well, not her. No, it was nothing to do with her.' He pulled away, as if what he wanted was to be the one in charge of his hands, so many other people were running the rest of his life. 'This Ivy Stardust lot,' he confessed. 'They're coming on real heavy...'

Ellie nodded. She had guessed right; except, her knowing that didn't solve his problems. But perhaps the other thing she'd achieved at the pool might – and that whipped-dog look on his face had to have something done about it. 'Well, a couple of things,' she said. 'I said I'd got a bit of news to tell you, to cheer you up, but there's more than that...'

'Oh, yes?' He wasn't with her any more, he really wasn't.

'Well, the first thing is −' and here she took a deep breath − 'I think the police know about the Friday night racket. Don't ask me why, but I really think they know.'

He raised his face slowly to look at her. 'Why? How? What evidence have you got for that?' But he was getting up, pulling away, spiralling about in the kitchen. 'Where the hell does that leave us, if the police know about it?' Now he started to pace, for all the world looking as if he was about to have a panic attack. The kitchen chair scraped on the tiles as he pulled it to him and threw himself down again, his head in his hands, leaning on the table. He took some deep breaths as she put an arm around his back. 'Ellie, I've had a visit, and I'm not saying who from, but we do nothing, you hear? We speak to no one, we keep ourselves to ourselves. No one in this place has got to make a move... For reasons! *Reasons!*' he shouted, shaking her off. He got up again and went to the back door and banged his head on it, stopping just short of violence.

'From who? You've had a visit from who?' She followed him. 'From the Watsons? About her being ill? I know that!'

He was facing her, and he was crying now. 'Heavier,' he said. 'Heavier, real threatening...'

242

Ellie was hugging her father now, speaking between the racks of his breathing. 'What did they say?'

He pulled away. 'We do *nothing*!' he shouted at her, except his voice had no sound to it this time, his words were only so much breath. 'Except sell up and move!'

There was a rap on the kitchen door. Annie put her head round. 'I'm off now, guv'nor,' she said, ignoring the commotion. 'See you tomorrer.'

Chris Searle's back was to her, he had spun away fast.

'Yeah, okay,' Ellie said.

'You gonna be all right?' Annie frowned. 'He don't look well, girl.'

'Hay fever,' Ellie said. 'Allergy.'

'Must be me!' Annie said – and she headed for the door. 'Me husband's got a dose of that.'

Ellie's dad went for the sink and sluiced and spat, and came up red and wet, looking like something newborn. 'I'll have to get in that bar.'

Ellie grabbed at him again, and shook him, took a deep breath and raised her voice a tone. 'Yeah,' she said, 'you get in that bar, Dad, and you do your job – and you don't worry about anything else, because everything else is going to be all right. You don't sell, you don't move. We're gonna win – you trust me on this.' She kissed him on a cold cheek, and pushed him to the door of the bar, where Annie's customer was heading out. Sky Sports played high up on one wall, commentary, commentary, commentary; if only things could be like that, Ellie thought, winning, walking off a pitch or a court or a wicket all right and triumphant; or just losing, like normal people lose – it's not the end of the world. What was that feeling like? She had long forgotten.

But as she went upstairs to change, she had grave doubts about the state of her dad, and about that 'keep-it-schtum' policeman – was her dad lying, and the policeman was the one putting the real frighteners on, in the pay of the Watsons? Well, she knew already that she'd be outside tomorrow night, looking for him. He'd been on the towpath twice before. She wanted another word with him – and if she wasn't satisfied, she *was* going to walk in through the door of Limehouse Police Station.

She was in her bedroom before she remembered that she hadn't told her dad her other piece of news: what she'd decided she was going to say to Mrs. Moses. But, then, how much difference was that likely to make any more?

Off Cleve Marshes, in the mouth of the River Swale, Hector McLeish cut off his engines and dropped anchor. Down inside, the cabin decking of the Laughing Lady *was covered by a plastic sheet, and one by one the Chinese* were brought up, bedraggled, from the bilge. *Song was dirty again, smelly with oil this time, but she soon found that McLeish had a routine, he knew a spot where his passengers could strip off without being seen, on the lee side of the boat, and dunk themselves in the Thames Estuary. From the look on his face it was a part of the operation that gave him pleasure, a sense of power when Song again had to lose her modesty. When she hesitated before going into the water, he gripped her so tightly that he marked her, and he smiled into her face.*

'In ye go, lassie!'

All their clothing except their shoes was bundled into a black plastic sack, weighted with two old anchor shackles, and dropped overboard when the boat returned to the shipping lanes. Song was thrown fresh clothes by Myra McLeish, men and women together in the main cabin, all the curtains at the portholes drawn closed, as they would stay from now on. Everyone kept their backs to everyone else as they all dressed quickly.

'Now ye won't get picked out by your smell!'

They were fed, and the Laughing Lady *went on up the Thames. Song sat silent, wondering who had worn these clothes before; who else had lost their identity in the hands of these people?*

As night fell the boat slowed, the engine revved back, and the woman opened the trap to the bilge again, ready just in case. Song eyed the small opening with disgust; and her heart raced, they were coming to a crucial final part of their journey. From outside she heard the hooting of a car, and the roar of an aeroplane, shouts from people very close who had to be on a jetty; and then the rattle of the anchor chain as the boat came to a mooring. Song looked around the cabin. Sitting along the facing lockers, there wasn't a single joyful expression among the Chinese to say that their journey into England was over, that they were here.

As soon as the sailing cruiser was moored, Hector McLeish ducked himself into the cabin. 'Gi yourselves a wee cheer inside, then!' he told them. 'You made it, you're in England now, which isnae Scotland, I grant ye – but it's where you wanted to be.'

Song didn't look to see whether or not the others were smiling at this, she was staring at her feet. So, she was here, this was England – and she had been brought in like a criminal. Somehow, she had thought from Uncle Chen that she would have been given papers at the last, and been able to walk with clear eyes past an officer at a desk. What a fool she was!

'What will happen now?' asked Lao Zi.

'Now we wait,' Myra McLeish put in. 'Waity-waity, you savvy?' She pointed down at the boat's floor, which Song hoped didn't mean that foul bilge again.

246

'Here in the boat,' the Scotsman made clear. 'In a wee while you'll be delivered to your next boat, then it's to your bosses, some of yous here, some there, all over this green and unpleasant land.' He eyed them around the room, every one, waiting till each pair of eyes met his. He was a strong man, Song had felt his force as he had made her swim, and he had that twist to his mouth that spoke of spite. 'And you'll behave yourselves. You'll do what you're told in England –' and he looked especially at Song – 'whatever you have to do, ye're goin' to have to do it!'

Song's spirits dropped even lower. She had been so stupid to think that she would have the chance to sing in concerts here in England. Of course she had known that it wouldn't happen straightaway, but the truth of it was, she was no more than a slave – it would never happen. They had all been treated like slaves getting here, and now they were going to be enslaved to hard bosses in England, who would rule their lives. Nothing that she had gone through, and nothing that lay ahead, seemed at all like the long but happy journey to opportunity in the West that Uncle Chen had talked about. Now she sat in the curtained cabin feeling sick, and betrayed. From the abduction of Tsai Fung, she had begun to suspect that she was no more than goods, property, with no rights. With the murder of Lin she knew. She would have to do whatever these people told her to do: and who knew what that might be!

Song went on staring at her feet: but they were her feet, not their feet, and she was overwhelmed with outrage, and sadness. How could she have come to this? She saw her mother's loving, hopeful face – and she suddenly felt the gorge rise in her throat – and a numbing nausea that threatened to spill her last meal onto the cabin floor.

'Toilet!' she cried across to Myra McLeish, desperately holding a hand over her mouth.

'You know where the heads are.'

Song got up and ran. The heads were through a small doorway to the fore of the boat. She hurried for it, took herself quickly inside and locked the door, inhaling the strong smell of disinfectant – which only made things worse. She just had time to lift the lid covering the seat when a great heave sent her half-digested food down into the pan.

And with her food, it seemed, had gone all her hopes. She lifted her head, her eyes bleary with tears, her body holding off taking in a deep breath while she waited to see if she had finished retching, staring up at the porthole so as not to have to look. The porthole glass was misted, opaque. She hadn't even seen anything of this new world yet, her one-time land of hope. She paused before going to wash her mouth out. Was the porthole open, so she could at least see where she was?

She lifted a hand to it; and it was open, and so well-oiled that it gave to her easily and made no sound. She looked out. She was in a sort of dock, or basin, with other boats and long narrow barges moored. Around her were tall buildings, smart, a lot of glass reflecting the evening lights; which meant many windows, so she kept her head well back, not to be seen. And from this slightly further perspective, she opened the porthole wider – but suddenly found herself looking not through it at the view, but at the brass-rimmed aperture itself.

It was just big enough for a slim, lithe body to get through!

She didn't ponder; she had only a short time in here before someone came to knock at the door. She shook off her shoes and climbed onto the lavatory seat. From here, bent over, she squeezed her right arm through the aperture, and her head, just; and where the shoulders go, the rest of a slim body should. With a catch of her breath, and a push, and a wriggle, and a pull on the lowest rail of the deck above her, she wormed her way through the porthole, to hang down the side of the boat with the backs of her legs against the inside of the heads, holding her in place for a second. She had to go now, because there was no going back! With a small touch of the lucky ceramic *peach hanging over her face and taking a deep breath, she let herself drop, to dive with hardly a splash into the water of Limehouse Basin.*

Who knew where she'd surface? But it couldn't be a worse place than the boat she'd just come from.

CHAPTER THIRTEEN

Flo still wasn't the old Flo, not the first Flo that Ellie had sat next to in the form room – but neither was she the Flo who didn't seem aware that Ellie Searle existed. She was somewhere between the two, giving the feeling that it wouldn't take much to bring the two of them together again.

There was a sign, if it could be read as a sign, in PE at the end of the afternoon when they finished the lesson with a game of handball in the gym. When teams were picked for the match on pitch three, where Flo had been made one of the captains, she thought long and hard about the selection of her first player, and, 'Ellie Searle,' she said, pointing but not looking at Ellie. And Ellie had to fight really hard not to say 'thank you', but just to saunter over as if it was only natural that she should be Flo's first selection.

But, better still, Flo came to the Regent's Arms that Friday night. Ellie hadn't dared hope that she would – although she wasn't mega surprised when she did: there had been signs. Okay, unspoken words still lay between them – and there was something important to be said to Mrs. Moses – but, one step at a time.

The Moses women came early, both looking good: *see what trouble we've taken?* was the message that night.

'Snazzy outfit!' Ellie said to Flo. The girl was wearing a velour tracksuit top and a short white skirt.

Flo looked at her, just a hint in her eyes of *what do you expect from quality like me?* 'You're not so bedraggled yourself!' Ellie was in a T-shirt with a long black skirt and thick boots.

Chris Searle, who had spruced himself up a bit, smiled weakly at Mrs. Moses when in truth her appearance deserved a round of applause.

'I brought some new stuff tonight,' she said. 'That all right with you, boss man?'

252

'Sure.'

'It's easy – garlic dough sticks for going in the oven, battered strips of courgette, an' chicken Cajun, all finger food...'

'No rolls?'

'No rolls. Let's educate them. Ed-u-cate! For the future!'

She was so upbeat that Ellie suddenly felt ashamed of her father's lack of appreciation. Surely he could say something! 'Really great!' she said, for him. 'Just the sort of thing to make the Regent's Arms special.' Okay, it was over the top, but Mrs. Moses gave Ellie a look, as if she knew what Ellie was doing; and a little smile came – just having heard the answer to the question put the week before.

'Then we get ready!' she said. 'You girls goin' to help?'

'Aprons out!' Ellie led the way into the kitchen, with her heart thumping fast for more reasons than she could ever explain.

She and Flo began standing side by side, unwrapping the food that Mrs. Moses had brought in with her. They listened to Mrs. Moses' instructions and then carried trays over to the oven, which meant standing aside for each other – 'after you', 'excuse me' between the girls – all polite and artificial. Until, while Ellie was putting in her final tray, Flo suddenly said, 'Would you mind getting your fat arse out the way?'

So Ellie wiggled it to annoy, and Flo kicked it – and her trayful of dough sticks slid to the floor.

'Stupid! You stupid girl!' Mrs. Moses shouted at her.

The three of them looked down at the damage. Luckily, most of the dough sticks had stayed on the tray, but a few from the edge were rolling across the tiles. Mrs. Moses scooped up the tray and thrust it at Flo. 'Get them in the oven – an' throw them others in the bin!' Ellie had never seen such big eyes on Flo's mother. The woman stood tall, and breathed in noisily through her nostrils, and finally told them, 'Why don't you two lose yourselves? You're all right on your own, but together you're a disaster!'

'Come on, disaster,' Flo said – 'I can't work in an oppressive atmosphere.' And led the way out of the kitchen. 'Opp-ressive!' she said, back over her shoulder as they headed for the outside door.

The music was nearly ready. The heavy speakers were being joggled into place by the two tough guys, Len Stevens was running arpeggios up and down his keyboard, Rude Boy Watson was busy selling tickets at the door, and Ivy Watson was taking off her coat and smoothing her long, low-cut dress, while Chris Searle silently lined up his glasses and checked on his pumps and optics, choosing not to look at the man who'd threatened him with a knife. To Ellie there wasn't the same 'on top' attitude from the Watsons as there'd been the week before, but there was still that bullying sense of ownership, a 'this is our place' arrogance about them all as they took the place over. Rude Boy ignored Ellie, stared at Flo, forgot even to waggle his tongue. But Ellie wasn't concerned with him that minute, she was too full of what had just happened.

Flo had started treating her the way she used to; Flo had kicked her up the bum for a laugh – a laugh! An old laugh!

It was too chilly to go out without coats, but they went, anyway. The days were shorter now, and although there was still some light left in the sky, the lamps were lit up on the roadways. Downstream, the smart apartments of Limehouse Basin shone out, and overhead the Friday night procession of flashing airliners headed, minute after minute, for Heathrow. Moored just above the lock, the *Watson Travel* cabin cruiser was tied up and unloading, and, upstream of it, two narrowboats were sitting by the towpath, smokestacks pluming, which had Ellie's eyes sharp for that policeman – that was where he'd been nosing before – although her ears were alert to whatever was going to be said by Flo. And, somehow, it had to be Flo who spoke first.

'Do you know anything about me?' Flo suddenly asked,

as she led them down towards the arched bridge over the canal.

'Like what?' Ellie asked.

'Like *anything* about me?'

On the first day of term Ellie would have made up something outrageous to say and got the Flo Moses shriek, dishing out punch for punch, fighting fire with fire, but things were very different now. 'You mean, where you come from, who your dad is, why you and your mum are on your own...?' No, she didn't know anything about Flo, but these were definitely questions she had asked herself over the weeks, important questions once the Chris Searle and Madeleine Moses thing had sparked off.

'You got it. All that personal stuff, leave out SATs an' cycling proficiency...'

Ellie thought about what she did know. Flo had always seemed to close up when they got talking about anything really personal, except that her mother worked in a West End big-store canteen and wanted to be more local. Whatever facts were known between them were all on Ellie's side; she had never been invited to Flo's home, wouldn't know how to find it, even. 'Dunno. You're a woman of mystery. You could be an apparition.'

Flo didn't whoop. Instead, she leaned against the brickwork under the bridge, and Ellie leaned beside her.

'Right. Me. Florence Edith Moses,' she said. 'But

that's *her* surname; his was Beckford, they never got married, her and my dad. An' I've got no sisters, no brothers, an' he was a small-time croupier – on the cheap tables...'

'A what?'

'A croupier,' Flo repeated flatly. 'He dealt cards in crappy casinos, threw little balls into roulette wheels.'

'Ah.'

'An' he was a real load of fun! The biggest laugh. He did magic an' stuff with me, made me his princess, worked nights so he took me all over in the days, all the London places. We was a pair,' she held two fingers together, 'Freddie an' Flo, you could hear us laughing all the way down the street.' Although Ellie would never believe it, judging by the croaky voice telling her this.

Flo swallowed. 'An' then he went. I was ten, an' he went off with some dancer who'd slid off a pole. Went out the door jingling his change in his pocket an' never came back.'

'Oh.'

'An' while I pined after him, always hoping, looking up and down the street at his regular early morning times for coming in, we got poorer, got chucked out of our house, an' my mum had to work like stink to bring the money in, plus done her level best to be the dad that my dad had stopped bein'...'

'She would.'

Flo pulled herself up off the wall and looked both ways along the towpath, then down at her shoes, before slumping back against the brickwork. 'An' then one day she met this other guy. Nice. White, as it goes. Supervisor at her job, south London,' no look at Ellie, 'wore one of those white trilby hats around the food an' doffed it when she walked in, mornings.'

Again, Ellie swallowed – because could she see what was coming?

'An' he done his best to be mates with me – but I wasn't having it, was I? I saw him off, fastest. It was too quick, what they was doin'. I didn't want him around my mum when there was any chance my dad was gonna walk back in an' say sorry. Which she would've accepted, after some enormous row.' Flo stopped speaking for a long while. Above them, traffic ran over the bridge, a Docklands Light Railway train headed into Limehouse Station, and up and beyond a 747 roared low towards the airport. 'I did everything in the book to make that thing not work…' And Ellie could see that Flo's eyes were filling with tears. She had never thought Flo could cry, but the girl was very close to it now. 'An' he never came back, not my dad, Freddie Beckford – he went off to South Africa, loads of casinos out there – and not Mr. Nice White Guy, he never came back neither.'

Ellie left Flo to her moment, didn't interrupt by saying something comforting and crass.

'So that, Chicken, is why this girl didn't dump on you.' Flo came closer. 'Because I've been there. I know the feeling you're feeling, remembering your mum from not long back, not wanting someone new, not yet, an' I regret what I done, the way you –' She left her words echoing under the bridge.

'Regret what *I've* done.' Ellie was nodding. She reached out a hand to touch Flo's.

'It would have been better all round if I hadn't seen that guy off. Me flouncing about, not giving 'em peace, making it transparent I didn't like him being near my mum. He was good for her, an' we wouldn't be living in the pits we're living in now...'

Ellie walked a few paces away, thinking. It was all so complicated. So did Flo want her mother to be friendly with Ellie's dad to do better for themselves, was that why Flo hadn't turned on her?

But Flo came after her; seemed to have realized how this had all come out. 'Don't get me wrong – you can keep your pub, Chicken. You can keep your dad, if that's why you think I didn't want to lose you. It's not that, honest, it's just, I've been where you've been. Yours died; mine died in here...' She poked at her heart.

Ellie turned to her.

Flo wiped her eye. 'I've seen my mum so depressed that I've had to push her out of her bed, I've had to find her knickers, put her shoes on for her, and make sure she went out the door to go to work. Some weeks I've done all the cooking indoors – and I've been down Stratford to buy her that black hat to wear, to spronce her up – an' forced her into buying that suit.' Flo nodded to herself. 'An' then your dad made all the difference. You an' me friends, the pub, the chance of a job, an' his smile and blue eyes. She turned into a different woman, ol' Madeleine Moses...'

Ellie put her hands on Flo's shoulders. Her own eyes were filling with tears. 'That's the only reason I went for Jaz,' she said. 'Not *against* you, more holding you off, 'cos I really reckoned it was still too close to what had happened...' Suddenly, she shook her friend. 'But it isn't really!' she said. 'Your mum would be so good for my dad...' There! She'd said it.

Flo stared back. 'You reckon?'

'I reckon.'

And the two girls threw themselves into each other's arms and hugged tight. Until Flo pulled off. 'Chicken, I'm real glad about that,' she said, 'because I didn't want no enemy for a little sister.'

Cars went on drumming above, another aircraft went over; and upstream the first testing sounds of the Ivy Watson acoustics were heard. But *what* had Flo just said?

'What do you mean, *little* sister?' Ellie asked. She'd guessed where things could lead ever since the second night with them all together at the Regent. 'Sister' she didn't mind, but, *little*? 'When's your birthday?' she demanded.

'April the fourth.'

'And mine's January the twenty-sixth. *You're* the little sister, my friend.'

'Oh, no!' Flo came back. 'Not everywhere!' – and stuck out her chest and shrieked, the old shriek.

And suddenly Ellie wanted to let her tears roll, and only just held it off because Ivy's music had begun ringing out over the canal. And her first song this time? 'These Foolish Things'. Where 'cigarette' was the second word, right up front tonight, getting a cheer and a clap from the pub. And just didn't the sound of that third-rate voice get under the skin! She swallowed her emotion: she had to push her personal stuff to one side, because here they were again, the bullying Watsons, their nicotine-yellow fingers back in the pot. Flaunting their racket.

'Come on,' she said, pulling Flo with her. 'They're doing it! We were right, they're definitely selling dodgy cigarettes...'

'Brains! Told you!'

'And my dad'll get caught up in it – bound to – and I'm not having that!'

'Chicken, what we gonna do?'

'I'll tell you.' And Ellie had noticed the 'we'. 'You make sure for yourself while I go looking for someone...'

'Who?'

'Tell you in a minute.' Shivering, they ran back into the warmth of the Regent's Arms, with such innocent faces on that they'd have been read as suspicious by a good psychologist. And one pair of eyes *was* reading them that way; someone's unblinking stare was fixed on Ellie as she and Flo went back into the bar. It was a man with a scowl and a foul yellow cigarette, sitting by himself across the room, with Len Stevens's eyes on him in turn – and whose presence could have been the reason for Ivy Stardust doing what she did right then, ending her first set to get the business going. He didn't blink as Ellie went for the door marked 'Private' to grab her coat, but when she headed with the smokers for the door to the towpath, he got up, and, taking his time, followed after her.

Outside, Ellie knew she had to find that policeman. She hoped like hell that the man was somewhere around tonight – and that he could be trusted. Being here would mean he was taking things seriously, and she could demand to know when he was going to take some action. But if he wasn't here, it would mean he probably *was* bent, turning a blind eye to what was going on.

She headed downstream first, towards the lights of the

Basin and its apartments. A quick check here, and then she'd go upstream to where they'd met him before, near the moored narrowboats. He could be anywhere, if he was keeping watch.

But what was this? Just along the towpath someone was at the canal side – climbing up out of the water, a woman in a clinging, drenched dress, her hair hanging down in willows, getting up onto her feet on the bank, and starting to run towards her, the water flying off her like fantasy in the lights. *Who was this?* It was a sight, a vision of Ophelia, out from her watery grave. *Or was it a vision of someone else?* Because there for an instant, Ellie thought that she saw…her mother.

She stood, iced, her head light with a supernatural question. Her mother was dead. *So was this her ghost, was this her dead, drowned mother?*

What stupid nonsense! The soaking wet female running barefoot at her was more like a girl than a woman, and not much older than she was – but Chinese or Vietnamese. And in trouble.

The girl grabbed at Ellie, pleading, 'Help me! You will help me? Please?'

'You fallen in?' Ellie asked. 'You want some dry clothes?'

'Hide! Hide me!' The girl turned, shivering, frightened, peering back through the tunnel. 'Bad people!'

'Bad people chucked you in?'

The girl shook her head, clutching at Ellie's shoulder. 'I escape!' she said. 'Please be my friend. Do not let them take me back!' She stroked Ellie's arms, her eyes pleading. 'Friend?'

And something about that word right now, together with those thoughts of her mother, went to Ellie's heart. *Friend.* Yes, she could be a friend — a good friend as well as a bad friend.

'Please!' The girl looked over her shoulder again — and now Ellie could see the figure of a man — a big man — running towards them, not shouting, as if it were a secret chase, spooky. Ellie shot a look over her own shoulder, and coming out of the pub the other way was a scary, hard-looking man, pushing past the smokers in the doorway.

'Quick!' Ellie said. 'Up here!' She twisted the girl around and pushed her back a few metres, to where a flight of steep steps led up to a block of apartments. Up here were bright lights, and doors to bang on for help. But when they got up there, the outer doors to the apartments were grilled and shut against Friday night, and there was no time for frantic pushing at an entryphone. Ellie stared this way and that. Opposite the block was a line of concrete tubs holding conifers, and she knew from walking this way that there was space between them and a high wall. It was a chance – and the only chance, because running on would only take them around the block and back to the Basin, a dead end.

'Here! Down here!' Ellie hissed, dragging the Chinese girl over and pushing her down behind the tubs. 'Crawl! Get along to the end!' She urged the girl on: further along there was less light.

The girl crawled as far as she could, and lay there panting noisily, but there were cars and aeroplanes to cover the sounds of the state she was in. Ellie pulled herself along and lay down behind her, making herself as small as she could, covering her face with the hood of her coat to show no pale skin – laying still, no muscle moving except the pounding muscle of her heart. And then, nothing. After the frantic panic everything went quiet, and there was the wait, the terrifying wait running up to finding out whether the hiding place had worked, or hadn't. Where the steps from the towpath led up here was a dark recess, and there was just a chance that they hadn't been seen taking the turn – while there were bushes and shrubs all along the towpath where they could have gone.

Ellie still didn't move as the girl began to quieten in her breathing, controlling her wet shivers. But now was always the worst time in hide-and-seek, when you can't see out, when you don't know if anyone's getting nearer.

Time hangs, seconds seem like minutes, you always need to pee, and just when you think it's all clear, you come out into the arms of the seeker, who's been silently prowling your patch. And this seemed so much more serious for the girl than any kids' game. The way she'd run at Ellie, there was no question that she was running for her life.

Ellie counted a hundred; then another hundred. She said, 'Ssssh!' quietly along to the girl, in case she wanted to make a move too soon; but the girl was making no sound now, was lying as still as a corpse. And then Ellie heard it, the scrape of a shoe, close by. There'd been no sound from the steps, no voices, no heavy breathing like a chasing man might make — but now she heard the sinister scrape of a shoe, near, very near. She froze, under her heavy clothes her body seemed to turn itself inside-out. She stopped breathing altogether, although she knew that when she had to breathe again it would be noisy; so she tried to control it, short, slight, panting breaths, all the while her ears within her muffling hood listening for another scrape. Which could be even nearer, prowling by the pots, or, please God, further away, giving them a dog's chance.

But the voice, when it came, was close. Too close, and right above them. 'This way,' a man said, 'she came by this way...' It was a Scotsman, deep and angry.

'No!' Another voice, foreign sounding.

Oh, yes! Please, God, would he lead the other man away, then?

'Not *she. Them.* Two. Two to find!'

Ellie didn't know that a frozen, frightened body could have any more fright heaped upon it, but she was in an avalanche of fear. Terrified. This second man's voice sounded so dangerous, like all the stalking killers a nightmare could throw up. And the Chinese girl along in front of her had stiffened, too, Ellie sensed it.

'Wormed herself out of the heads,' the Scotsman said. 'Spun us the yarn that she was sick...'

'Five minutes. Five minutes. You bring the rest,' the second man said. 'Many people there; this is best time.'

'Aye.'

'Eight, they pay for. They want eight! You bring others!'

'Sure. After we nab this one!'

And now Ellie's mouth dropped open. Was the Regent's Arms involved in a hell of a lot more than smuggled cigarettes? Was it part of an illegal immigration network? Was this hard man out there a big part of the racket, in charge? It seemed like the Scotsman was scared of him. Their voices and the sounds of their shoes were coming and going. Ellie's frantic brain saw them checking on the entrance to the apartment block, and maybe further along the walkway. But whenever the sounds faded, they came back near.

'Not to lose in London. We lose, she talk, we are finished,' the killer voice growled. There was the sound of a loud hawk and a spit and a vehemence of foreign swear words. 'So we find!' He shouted it – and suddenly the fronds of the firs above Ellie were pushed aside by violent hands – and when she twisted her head to look up, there was his face staring down at her. His pale and violent face.

'Help!' Ellie shouted. 'Dad! Police! Someone help!' She tried to get up and run, but the man was at her, at the entrance to their narrow tunnel and dragging her out – and before she could open her mouth to shout again, a foul nicotine hand was clamped across her mouth and nose. She couldn't breathe, she was being suffocated as he dragged her to her feet. The Chinese girl was trying to make a run for it, but the big Scotsman had got her, too, and her mouth also was clamped into silence.

'You take!' the man holding Ellie said to the other. And in a swift and skilful move by people who had to be so used to manhandling others, she and the Chinese girl were thrown across, swapped by the two men. 'I go to barges, wait for the rest. You take this!' – which meant Ellie. 'Sort! Go to boat! Sort in deep water!' The foreign man took the Chinese girl. He had his arm around her, the hand still over her mouth. She kicked and pushed and pulled, but he was a powerful man, and he dragged her back towards the towpath, no problem, and carried her struggling down them.

Where Ellie was forced to follow. 'C'mon, ye stupid, interfering child!' There was no getting away from him. He held her tight, one hand around the shoulders, and the other over her mouth, yanking her down the steps to the towpath; and, with no people along this far, marching her unseen towards the Basin.

Sort in deep water? Ellie knew what that meant! Money had been paid for that Chinese girl, she was *property*: whatever was going on was big business. These were violent men and now she herself was in their way, and she was going to be taken down the Thames, to be thrown overboard well out at sea. All this going through her head in a flash as she kicked, she struggled, she tried to scream – but there was nothing she could do. The man was too strong. She was in his clamp, she was helpless, and she was going to end up like lots of people who cross gangsters in London end up – dead. Drowned, like her mum.

He was dragging her now, along the towpath and towards the Basin quayside, towards the boat that was going to be a coffin ship for Ellie Searle. She gave another almighty twist, but the Scotsman had her in a powerful grip, which he'd altered a bit in case anyone was looking. And he was holding his cheek close to hers as if he might be saying something sweet — while he stopped her speaking herself.

Except that in the last struggle and the change of his grip, suddenly, in the thickness of her coat and with the slimness of her body, Ellie found a couple of millimetres of space, and with a quick, surprising duck she was out from his clamp: free for a second — to run for her life.

The man came charging after her — but Ellie had two metres on him, and she ran the only way she could, towards the Basin. Which was a dead end for her. She knew it was! There was nothing ahead but the water, and the man was gaining on her, grabbing at her. So there was no choice. Before last week she would have frozen — but now she knew she had to jump for it, jump in, and go under, there was no question of any other way. She zigzagged, her mind made hopelessly up, ran to the quayside edge, and without a pause she vaulted the loop of chain to jump — as far out as she could — into the deep water of Limehouse Basin.

You never hear your own splash, but you feel the shock as the world changes. She was hit by the cold to the face, and dragged down by the force of her jump, pulled deeper by her coat and her leather boots. She flailed, she struggled, she tried to kick and swim, but there was nothing for it, she went down fast beneath the surface, she hadn't the strength to kick against the weight of her clothing – and she knew then that there was no coming up.

This was how her mother had died, and this was how she would die: she was doing the Scotsman's work for him. But after the first strugglings, still holding her breath but getting no nearer the surface, all at once she was overcome by a strange and lucid calm. Weirdly, there was no panic. She knew where she was, she knew what was happening to her, and she knew that there was nothing she could do about it. She was going to be with her mother in a watery grave. In a strange, peaceful way she was content; water held no fear for her any more. This was how it had to be. She felt close, at one with the mother who had died underwater before her. And now, having held her breath for longer than she could ever have thought possible, now was the time to open her mouth and let the end happen. To open her mouth and say, *I'm here.*

To be suddenly gripped around the body again by strong arms. Ellie forced her eyes open in the dark water and kicked and struggled against this evil man. *Let me go! Let me go to my mother!*

But the hands around her were skilled and powerful, and she was flotsam in them. Suddenly, she broke surface, let out her held breath to scream – and was blinded by floodlights from the quay. She started to struggle again, but the voice in her ear was not Scottish. It was London. It was lifesaver. It was policeman.

'Easy! Easy!' he said; 'I've got you, Ellie! Struggle again and I'll have to duck you!'

Ellie stopped struggling. She lay on her back with her chin in the policeman's palm, eyes to the dark sky, being taken to the side.

'I reckon that's got me my Bronze Medallion!' the policeman said, as his colleagues fished her out. 'With ribbons on...'

Ellie lay gasping on the quayside, water running from her neck, from her sleeves, her boots; her long skirt flopping heavy on her legs. And there amid the confusion of police in their chequered baseball caps, was her father, who pulled her lovingly to her feet and wrung out the water with the huge intensity of his hug.

'The girl!' Ellie chattered. 'The Chinese girl!'

'We've got all eight of them,' the shirt-sleeved policeman said, doing his own stamping and shaking out of Basin water; shivering now. 'And Ivy Stardust'll be singing her songs in prison!'

'My wet Chicken...' Flo came to Ellie to hug and kiss her – against the background of shouting and swearing and jostling as the pale, hard-looking man and the

Watson suspects were being taken up to the police vehicles in Salmon Lane.

But Flo's was a voice – and using a pet name – that sounded so good to Ellie's ears.

CHAPTER FOURTEEN

The pub was empty of customers. By eleven o'clock that night, Ellie was in dry clothes sitting around a table with her dad, and Flo, and Mrs. Moses. And the policeman, in her dad's tracksuit.

'Lew,' he told them. 'Lew Birch.'

There was little sign that the Watsons and their gang had ever invaded the Regent's Arms. The speakers had been taken as scene of crime evidence, and the card table at the door had gone: the Regent's Arms was the Regent's Arms as Chris and Ellie Searle had first walked into it.

'Banged up!' Lew Birch was saying. 'They're all banged up tonight and for a good long time to come.'

'It was a hell of a lot more than the fags, then?' Ellie's dad asked.

Lew Birch took in a breath and blew it out loudly for exclamation. 'I'll say,' he said. 'Cover, the cigarettes were – smokescreen. See, bringing punters in to buy their cigarettes made this place look busy, put a lot of activity on the towpath, all those dedicated smokers going out for their gasps, it created what we call "footfall" to cover the real smuggling – which was people.'

Everyone around the table exchanged looks. This was the real, big stuff.

'Chinese people mostly, youngish. Poor devils. They pay fortunes over in China, or run up debts they can never repay, say goodbye to their families, and come to a sort of slavery over here.'

Ellie nearly said, 'That girl hiding with me, on the towpath, she was Chinese...' – but for some reason she didn't, although she didn't know why.

Lew Birch suddenly turned to her. 'And because you got me my Bronze Medallion, young lady, I'll show you how it was done. All of you – you can all come!' He got up, with a clearing of his throat; and Ellie knew very well what he was saying: she was special to him, she always would be, someone whose life you've saved *has* to be. Pushing a couple of chairs aside, he led them out to the towpath, to the first of the two narrowboats, which was guarded by a uniformed policeman. 'It's all right, Tom,' he said – 'we're not going right in.' He led them onto the afterdeck of the narrowboat, and opened the hatchway into the long cabin, letting Ellie look first.

And it was not at all as Ellie had imagined, all bunks and brass. Inside the empty cabin were tables set up like a floating office, with maroon British passports on one, and papers and rubber stamps on another, and at the far end a light was rigged up, and a white screen, faced by a camera on a tripod.

'They can take all the time they want, on a narrowboat, being leisure craft,' Lew Birch said. 'Even a photographer – we've nabbed her – for new papers and passports.'

'Going where?' Madeleine Moses asked. 'On this boat?'

Flo snorted; a comment on her mother's pushiness.

'I'll tell you, love, it's not Official Secrets stuff. The hardest part for these people is this bit, off the boats and into the transport system. We've got better surveillance at our ports and harbours and airports than anywhere else in the UK. So this lot avoid the real docks. They do the business under cover of Ellie's pub here...'

Ellie's pub! Thank you very much!

'...Then they use the canal to take them –' he held the moment, for Madeleine Moses' benefit – 'up to King's Cross, where there's a big canal place. And, of course—'

'The railway station,' Chris Searle said.

'With lines running north and west and east. They hop off this little number at King's Cross and onto trains carrying their new identities – to fool the farmers and keep the employment people happy. All legal. Looking.'

'Ah.' Every head nodded.

'Or, some of them might go on in one of these barges, Birmingham, Liverpool, wherever. I ask you, who stops and searches on the canals? Then it's pick the fruit, lift the spuds, dig for cockles, clean the fast food joints, do all the jobs the English don't want to do any more. For peanuts! Hounded by snakeheads, their wages snatched back to pay their debts for coming here, so it's years and years and years before they start sending any money home – if ever. What a life!'

Necks were aching now, with bending to see into the narrowboat. 'Except they're all locked-up right now!'

Ellie's thoughts went to that scared, half-drowned Chinese girl who would be sent back to where she'd come from. A terrible, wasted journey.

The group made its way back to the Regent's Arms; but Mrs. Moses stopped the DI on the towpath.

'Who would ever suspect an innocent little boat of having that forgery stuff in it?' she said.

'You did!' Flo said to the policeman. 'Didn't you?' Her eyes were big; well, she fancied herself CID.

'Sure. We've been on to it for a while. But we couldn't move till we knew we were moving on one of the Fridays when stuff was happening. The people stuff. Otherwise, we'd've shown our hand and frightened them off.'

'And the cigarettes?' Ellie asked. 'Am I right — do they come in on the roof of Watson's coaches, in the air conditioning?' She looked at the others, ready for her little bit of acclaim.

The policeman shook his head. 'That's the funny thing — they're not even bent cigarettes,' he said. 'Len Stevens buys them at the cash 'n' carry.' Big eyes again, between Ellie and her dad. 'They sell 'em cheap *like* bootlegged fags, but they're what business people call a "loss leader", part of their expenses to attract the crowd they want, to mask their other stuff, the people transfer from Basin to canal. Just miss the odd week to get a good crowd for an "immigrant" night...'

'And you knew about all this?' Madeleine Moses asked him.

Lew Birch smiled modestly. 'But I'm sorry you had to

get wet,' he told Ellie. 'We were staking it out tonight; we knew from the coastguard that this was a real shipment. They could tell from the boat's configuration and lie on the water. Dead suspicious, the customs man reckoned.'

Ellie's dad led them back into the Regent's Arms; and Ellie was pleased to see Annie there still, not arrested; she hadn't been in on the scam.

'So why didn't this coastguard bloke stop the boat there and then?' Flo asked, as Lew Birch knocked back a Scotch. 'Would've saved my mate here a swim!'

Lew looked across at Ellie, and smiled. 'We had to let them get to the Basin, and get the first Chinese illegal taken to a narrowboat, or we wouldn't have had the evidence to charge her owner. This way we've got the whole gang from the traffickers to the snakehead gangmasters to the boatmen living off these people.' He tapped his personal radio, then turned to Ellie's dad. 'And you nearly put the mockers on everything by trying to stop Ivy Watson's Friday nights!'

'My application?' Chris Searle asked.

'Dot Bartam's not only on the council planning committee,' Lew Birch said, 'she's on the police committee, too.'

But in all this explanation and congratulation, Ellie was sitting with her forefinger pushing around a small pool of spilled drink on the tabletop. It was in the shape of a curve – or a question mark. 'What about the girl?' she asked. 'The one who came out of the canal? What'll happen to her?' She felt responsible somehow for her, having tried to help her – and failed.

'What girl?'

'The one who was dripping wet!'

'A dripping wet girl? No, love, you were the only wet girl!' Lew Birch said. 'Wet and heavy in those clothes, I can tell you...'

'Wasn't any of the Chinese girls wet?' Ellie had to have it clear. 'The ones you caught?'

'Dry as a bone – and as frightened as hell is hot.' The policeman got up and moved from the table; he had to get back to the police station to do all the paperwork, but as he went he promised that the snakehead master over from France, the Scots and the Watson gang – including the kid Wayne on his way to Feltham juvenile – wouldn't be coming out of custody for a very long time.

'Who knows what'll be here by the time they do?' Chris Searle said.

Everyone looked at everyone else. But it was left to Ellie to say it. 'Perhaps a smart little Italian restaurant,' she found a measured voice from somewhere. '*The Bella Canale*, run by the fabulous four!'

And as one, the four looked at one another and put their hands into the centre of the table, holding them together – like in an unbreakable pact. Until Madeleine lifted her glass, and they all clinked to the new life, eyes into eyes into eyes, and not a dry one between them.

Chris Searle got up and walked to the door with the policeman. 'I'll never thank you enough for saving my girl's life,' he said.

'Oh yes you will,' Lew Birch said. 'You ought to see the pasta I can stash away. You're on my patch.'

Which made Ellie laugh, and then she cried – and Ellie Searle the publican's daughter didn't cry. But these tears weren't for herself. They were for another girl, who was still wet and shivering somewhere nearby. Free, though: free in London to make some sort of a new life for herself.

Which everyone has to do, from time to time.

For more exciting thrillers log on to
www.fiction.usborne.com

Tim Wynne-Jones

The Boy in the Burning House

Jim doesn't want to believe that his missing father has been murdered but Ruth Rose is determined to help him root out the truth – no matter how painful or dangerous it is.

"This classy teenage thriller really gets the heart pumping... Phew – it's hot!" *The Funday Times*

Shortlisted for the Guardian Children's Fiction Prize 2005
0 7460 6481 0   £4.99

The Survival Game

When Burl runs away into the Canadian wilderness, he must find a way to survive and escape his bullying father's dangerous games for good.

"Just about everything you could possibly want from a book." Graham Marks, Children's Editor, *Publishing News*

Winner of the Canada Council Governor General's Literary Award
0 7460 6841 7   £5.99

L.M. Elliott

Under a War-Torn Sky

Shot down on a mission, bomber pilot Henry Forester is alone in a treacherous land. Just nineteen years old, Henry is suddenly forced to use all his wits and courage in order to survive a dangerous journey across Nazi-occupied Europe. Desperate to get back to his family and the girl he now realizes he loves, Henry is forced to rely on the kindness of strangers and the cunning of the French Resistance. He faces some stark choices and ultimately has to decide whether he can take someone's life in order to save his own.

Inspired by true personal stories, *Under a War-Torn Sky* is a searingly emotional and gripping account of life behind enemy lines during World War II.

"This truly is a great read which shows the emotions and hardships of war. It is a gripping, suspense-filled read, which is hard to put down."   *Glasgow Sunday Herald*

Winner of the Borders Original Voices Award

0 7460 6731 3   £5.99

Carol Hedges
Spy Girl series

The Dark Side of Midnight

Jazmin Dawson is a super-cool secret agent with hi-tech kit and a hi-octane life of crime busting...in her dreams! In reality, Jazmin is a schoolgirl with a serious snack habit, whose biggest battles are with her maths homework.

But when Jazmin's mum, who *is* a spy, goes missing, Jazmin is sent to rescue her and finds herself at the centre of an international mystery, with a dangerous mission to infiltrate a rogue scientific institute.

0 7460 6750 X   £4.99

Out of the Shadows

Spy Girl Jazmin receives her second assignment: to befriend a crucial witness in a case of identity theft. But when the witness vanishes, Jazmin is pitted against powerful enemies in the race to find him.

0 7460 7083 7   £5.99